The Black Sunshine of Goody Pryne

THE BLACK
SUNSHINE OF
GOODY PRYNE

Sarah Withrow

A GROUNDWOOD BOOK
DOUGLAS & McINTYRE
TORONTO VANCOUVER BERKELEY

Groundwood Books / Douglas & McIntyre
720 Bathurst Street, Suite 500, Toronto, Ontario M5S 2R4
Distributed in the USA by Publishers Group West
1700 Fourth Street, Berkeley, CA 94710

We acknowledge for their financial support of our publishing program
the Canada Council for the Arts, the Government of Canada through
the Book Publishing Industry Development Program (BPIDP), the
Ontario Arts Council and the Government of Ontario through the
Ontario Media Development Corporation's Ontario Book Initiative.

This book was written with the help of funding from the
Canada Council.

 Canada Council Conseil des Arts
for the Arts du Canada

ONTARIO ARTS COUNCIL
CONSEIL DES ARTS DE L'ONTARIO

National Library of Canada Cataloging in Publication
Withrow, Sarah
The black sunshine of Goody Pryne / by Sarah Withrow.
ISBN 0-88899-477-X (bound).–ISBN 0-88899-577-6 (pbk.)
I. Title.
PS8595.I8455B53 2003   jC813'.54   C2003-902984-0
PZ7

Cover illustration by Francesca Chessa
Design by Michael Solomon
Printed and bound in Canada

For my sister, Anna

Chapter 1

Goody grabs the orange muffin and stuffs it through the rip in the side of her plaid windbreaker. She already has a pack of all-dressed chips and some Hot Tamales in there.

"What about some jerky?" I whisper to her.

She shakes her head and makes for the freezer. I shoot a look at Kent at the cash. He's picking at his long nails with the edge of a matchbook. I follow Goody.

"Come on," I whine, and my foghorn voice breaks. I catch the reflection of my little-boy chin in the plastic top of the freezer as Goody opens it. She passes me a blue Mr. Freeze and makes her way to the cash. I'm eyeing the jerky, trying to show Goody just how much it means to me. I can almost taste the mushy, meaty saltiness.

Kent looks at me. His dark hair hangs over one eye.

"Pay the man, Stevie," Goody says and walks out the door. I hear the screen door snap shut behind her.

Kent's staring down at me, waiting. I hate the guy's puff face. I scribbled him out of that picture in the year book where he has his arm around Bea Fong, who I worship but have no hope of getting. If I were two years older, a foot taller or had any pectorals whatso-ever, I might begin to consider talking to her.

"What's she owe you?" I ask Kent, opening Dad's tan leather wallet.

"Fifty cents, Squeak," he says, making a fist and rubbing his fingers against the palm of his hand in front of my face.

I hate it when they do that to my face. I slap two quarters on the counter and leave.

Freezies. Man, it's almost winter already. The thing'll stick to my tongue.

I walk around to the back parking lot where Goody's sitting on the dumpster eating the muffin and flipping through her log book. The freezie wrapper is already half empty beside her. The other half is splattered on the ground, like the bluebird of happiness just gobbed there. I take my freezie and squeeze it.

"It's half melted already," I say.

"Freezer's been broken for five months. What'd you expect?"

I rip it open with my teeth and suck the juice out.

"Why'd you get me blue?"

"Don't like it, don't eat it. It's the cheapest thing in

the store. You should be happy I didn't get cheese or chicken."

"I don't think freezies come in cheese flavor," I say, and she looks at me through the corners of her squinty eyes. She pulls something out of her pocket and throws it at me.

It's a stick of jerky.

"You are the master," I bow to her.

"You have to learn to trust me," she says.

"I trust you, all right. I trust you to act like the thief that you are."

"That's it. Give me back the meat." She shoves her open hand in my face and wiggles her thick fingers.

"Sucker," I say and take a step back. Goody wipes her hand on her sweat pants and flips her hair out of her face.

If it weren't for Goody's long blonde frizzy hair that cuts across her face sideways, you'd swear she was a guy. Well, maybe not, because she's got those big curvy lips, too. Sometimes I pretend she's a guy, though, because she's got that way about her.

Goody doesn't put it on. She doesn't make like everything she's got is everything you want like most girls. And it's not just because she looks like she swallowed a Volkswagen that I think that. I don't see her like that. I see her like she's, you know, Goody. I see her like she's going to make me laugh, and go on and on about outer space, and steal me some jerky. I see her like she's going to kick my ass for being an idiot.

Sometimes I wonder if it'd be the same with us being friends if she were a guy, but mostly the only time I remember that she's not one is when we have to go to the washroom at the movies and I can't go where she goes. That, and in gym class. Which reminds me.

"I'm going to kill that Max Revy," I tell her.

"I'll do it," she says, jumping up off the dumpster and shoving her black star log in the big front pocket of her windbreaker. She's halfway across the parking lot before I start worrying she might really do it. She's been looking for an excuse to kick someone in the head. That's what she told me last week. She told me she wanted to feel what it'd be like to have a skull knock against her foot. Then she looked at my head like it might be a good candidate.

"Stop," I yell at her. She slows down but she doesn't stop.

You can never tell with Goody how serious she is.

I get this vibe off her, like it's only a matter of time before she bursts wide open and does something like you read about in the papers.

Most days I live in fear. Most days, all day long, I silently beg her to behave.

But occasionally this voice comes on in the back of my head and it's begging her the other way. It's cheering Goody on, dying for her to crack and burst and rain down on the world like grand finale fireworks.

"Come on, Goody. Stop. Please?"

She stops and takes the Hot Tamales out of her pocket. I jog over to her. We truck out of the parking lot and move past the screaming lime-green walls of Kent's family's store. It's called The Store Famous, but the only thing it's famous for is for being on the corner of Barrie and York Streets.

Goody stops in front of the store window, lifts the box of Hot Tamales above her head, opens her mouth and pours them in. Kent's standing right at the window watching her.

Goody says people don't notice anything unless it has to do with them personally. Like if you take someone's French fries they'll notice, but if you take someone's brother's French fries they won't.

I instinctively grab her wrist and pull it down.

"Stop it, Expletive," she says and lifts the pack up to her big mouth again.

I watch Kent's face. He's watching Goody but nothing registers. My heart's bouncing against my ribs like a tiny basketball. Kent looks over at me, makes me feel like I'm the one who stole stuff.

I can't breathe. I can't move.

He catches my eyes, narrows his, brings his hands in front of his face and rubs them together. In slow motion he mouths the word "Squeak."

I run the block to Skeleton Park without breathing. The cool fall wind whips at my throat down York Street. I head for my spot under the slide. I poke my hand into the hole between the platform and the slide and slip out one of my hidden swatches of blue cloth. I close my eyes and rub it on my forehead until I can hear Goody huffing her way toward me, then I whip it back to its spot.

"Did you think Kent was going to chase you down and bring you to justice? The proceeds of the crime was beef jerky, Stevie. I can't believe you left me there to take the rap after I stole for you. Lucky for you Kent's as gutless as roadkill."

Goody makes her way up the slide stairs. I can see her shoes between the slats of the platform. I punch the platform from underneath.

"That's effective," she mutters.

I hate her so much. I hustle out.

"Do you have to stick it to Kent like that?" I say, holding an imaginary box of Hot Tamales over my open mouth.

"It's my job. You know that, Stevie. Do you have to freak out like a weeny sucky weasel all the time?"

"You know that's my job," I say, and watch her grin. "Why do you hate him so much?"

"I don't hate him, exactly. I have great disdain for him. He's just at The Store Famous because his parents own the place. He doesn't know what a break he's getting. He's got money. He's got something to do. He's got his parents' trust and he shows contempt for it all by not even trying to catch me when he knows that I steal from him."

"So you show your disdain for him not catching you stealing by stealing more."

"The punishment should fit the crime. What do you care? You get what you want."

"He called me Squeak," I tell her, kicking at the sand in front of me. We both watch it hit the slide and fall down. Goody shrugs. She can't exactly get mad at Kent when she's the one who started calling me that. I made her swear not to do it anymore, but it doesn't stop everyone else.

"Sorry," she says, like she really is.

Goody's one of two people in the world and one in heaven who truly like me. The other alive person's my mother and, come to think of it, I'm not sure she truly likes me consistently, just on certain good days.

"Why are we going to kill Max Revy?" Goody asks.

"It was an expression. You know, like, oh my God,

I got mud on my white pants, my mom's going to kill me."

"Only in your case, your mom might actually kill you."

"She'd just tear up another picture of my dad."

"I really admire your mother's use of psychological tactics," Goody notes, licking Hot Tamale dust off her fingers.

I'm lucky my dad was good-looking or I'm sure Mom wouldn't have so many pictures of him to tear up any time I do something bad. I can tell she enjoys doing it, too. She's still pissed at him for dying young.

I was twelve when a drunk driver plowed into Dad's parked car in the bowling alley parking lot. Dad was sitting in the front seat finishing a stick of black licorice. We know that because they found half of it in his mouth and the other half in his hand. You'd think Mom would be mad at the drunk driver, but no, she says it's just the stupidest way to die she ever heard of and she blames my father one hundred percent for not fighting harder to stay alive. Lying in the coffin, his head didn't look bashed up, but the doctors said it got hit so hard that he died instantly. That was two years ago now, and I swear I haven't grown since.

I kick the sand again, watch it hit the slide and shush down.

"What did Max Revy do to you to make you say you'll kill him?" Goody asks.

"He called me Man Child in the locker room, all right? Satisfied?"

"You're the one who brought it up. Sounds to me like a perfectly accurate physical description," she says. I have to bite my lip on that one. I can tell she's waiting for me to say something physically accurate about her, like mega-mouth Josie Bissell does every chance she gets.

"Man Child is accurate, but unkind," I say.

"Unkind, but creative," she says. "You do look more eleven-ish than fourteen and, face it, you are on the scrawny side of skinny."

"Whose side are you on, anyway?" I hiss.

"Mine," she says, pulls a bag of chips from her pocket, squeezes them open and offers me one. "Come on, we'll fatten you up."

Talking with Goody is like tiptoeing through a minefield. But nobody knows the lay of the land better than me – except maybe Josie Bissell, Goody's ex-best friend. Josie pokes at Goody's mines with a short stick. You should see Goody's face when Josie has at her. It's like she's swallowing nails. Josie dares Goody to bust her. But Goody won't do it.

Last year I asked what happened between the two of them. "I promised Josie I wouldn't say anything about it," Goody said.

"But she hates you," I said, rubbing the swatch hidden in my mitt.

"She blames me for wrecking her life. Don't ask about it, Stevie, because I'm honoring my promise to her."

Goody and I were in the park that day, too. That was last winter, when the hockey rink was up. I remember the slide vibrating under my legs every time the hockey guys slammed the puck against the boards.

"Josie's always at you. Isn't she afraid you'll say something?"

"She's petrified. That's the best part. She's forced to trust her worst enemy with her biggest secret. She doesn't know if she can trust me, so every day she tests me out to see if my promise is still good. She lives in fear. It's really quite satisfying."

"You scare me," I told her, meaning to be funny. She closed her eyes and turned her head away. A puck hit the boards.

"I know," she whispered, just loud enough for me to hear.

The sky was bright blue that day. The winter sun made everything look sharp. I remember clearly because it's the only time I've seen Goody cry.

Chapter 2

When I get home, Mom's on the phone talking with my Aunt Lorraine about how disappointing their lives are. I don't think Aunt Lori is quite as disappointed as Mom is.

"And the guy wouldn't even open the door for me," Mom says to the phone.

She looks at me and points to the kitchen table, which means I'm supposed to set it. The stew's bubbling on the stove and its meatiness fills the warm air of the kitchen. I wander over and crack open the lid for a closer smell. And Mom's there immediately, swiping at my butt with a wooden spoon.

About the only gadget Mom ever bought was a longer cord for the phone so that she could cook and talk to Aunt Lori at the same time. It was cheaper than a portable phone. The two of them have got worse since the phone company came out with the new long-distance plans. Aunt Lori lives in Belleville, which is only forty-five minutes west of Kingston, but it's far enough that you have to pay to phone there. Now they talk for at least a couple of hours a night, and don't say anything about it unless you want to hear, in painful detail, how lonesome your mother is.

Mom's always on the phone between work and dinner anyway, so I hang with Goody and make up excuses why she shouldn't come to my house. My mom and Goody get along like they're sisters. I won't invite Goody over most of the time because it's like she's coming over to hang with Mom. They sit on the couch and make fun of me until they are both in hysterics. Once they laughed for half an hour over how my hair was smushed on one side after I'd been lying on the floor in front of the TV.

Goody doesn't think anyone on earth likes her except me and my mom, and that's only because she figures I have to like her because I'm a freak, and Mom is just crazy from grief.

Fortunately, I don't have to make up too many excuses because Goody's mom wants her at home early after school to do chores. Goody's dad lives across town with his new girlfriend. He's an English professor and the girlfriend is one of his former students. Needless to say, Mrs. Pryne is pretty pissed off at him and she takes it out on Goody by making her do chores.

Any time I ask about it, Goody just yells, "*Next subject.*" She never talks about her home at all, except to say about lying in this rubber raft she's put on the picnic table in her back yard. She spends all clear nights out there listening to her handcrank-powered radio, looking at the stars through her binoculars and recording things in the black log book that she carries with her everywhere – as if the stars might come out in the middle of the day and need charting. As if she's the one controlling the stars.

"I've got to feed this child, Lorraine, before his drool hits the floor." Mom hangs up.

"What's wrong with looking at food?" I ask her.

"Don't you start. If I have a lid on there, it's there for a reason. When you cook dinner you can look at the food all you like. Where are the forks?"

"It's stew, Mom. I put spoons."

She stands in the middle of the kitchen with the wooden spoon in her hand and looks about ready to burn or melt. One or the other. Her curly brown hair shivers against the snowy log-cabin wallpaper Dad picked out. She's small like I'm small and, like me, she has a wet-cat look when she's like this.

I go to the drawer to pull out the forks but it's already too late. She's melting. I hear the spoon fall to the floor and, next time I look, she's got both hands to her face. She waits until her long thin fingers are all wet and then she starts blubbering into the blue apron, all without moving from the exact middle of the kitchen.

It's not for cooking that Mom wears the apron. It's for being in this room where Dad used to sit at the end of the table nearest the stove, because he was cold, and he'd get in Mom's way and be of no use at all in the world.

I never know which way Mom's going to go. I used to be more careful about it. Now I just live knowing that something I'll say or do is going to tip her off to melting or burning, and I've got to be ready at all times for one or the other.

She doesn't lose it like this down on the Wolfe Island ferry where she works. I asked her why once. She was standing in my bedroom doorway on her way to bed.

"It's better out there," she said. "I can see far away. Here, I see too close."

"Maybe we should move, Mom," I said then, pulling my covers up a little to protect my chin. I'd been saving it to say, so my heart was pounding. If we moved, things would be better. They couldn't get any worse. I watched her and tried not to let it show on my face how bad I wanted her to say yes.

Instead, she said, "Oh, I could never do that." And that was that. She turned off my light from where she stood in the doorway. I watched her dark head turn into the light of the hall and caught the small smile on her face as she walked to the bathroom.

Now I walk up behind her, pull the apron from her eyes, guide her toward Dad's chair and gently push her into it. I pick up the spoon and get us each out some stew. I pour myself some milk and get a beer out for Mom. She looks at it and shakes her head, so I put it back in the fridge. Then I sit down and wait.

After a couple of minutes she blows her nose, picks up her spoon and tries a bit.

"I forgot to buy potatoes, Stevie. That's how come the dumplings."

"I like dumplings, Mom."

"They're good for getting the meat juice. How was your day, then?"

After dinner I head upstairs, take off my socks, lie down in the middle of my creaky bed and wait for my life to change. I've been waiting a long time.

I could try to make things better, like maybe learn to play the guitar.

At first that idea seems good and I start a great daydream about rocking out on stage with Eddie Vedder and then I can't hear the music, so the daydream switches to one where I'm riding up a Yukon mountain on my bike and I can feel the sweat on my face

and I can taste snow in the wind and I can see a thousand miles of mountain from how high up I am. Then I take a wrong turn and I land on my face with the air hammered out of my lungs while a humiliating laugh track plays in the background.

Tiny fish hooks reach into my brain and peel back the daydream. It curls back like a thin piece of rubber, and reality – big flat reality – lowers against the back of my eyes and I know, again, that the only reason I'm inventing a life is because I don't have one.

Chapter 3

Lunchtime, Wednesday. Sitting across from Goody in the cafeteria. Bea Fong is at the cash register paying for her lunch. I can see her whole tray. She's got vanilla pudding on there. She's the only girl in school who eats dessert.

I daydream that I'm smoothing the pudding along her arm, from the edge of her wrist to the inside of her elbow. In the daydream, I'm using a mini version of one of those plastic spatulas and I'm concentrating on the feel of the plastic on top of the pudding on top of Bea's arm and the weight of her hand in mine, because I'm holding it while I ice her with the pudding. I want to lick it off.

"Looking at the special of the day again?" Goody calls me back. I close my eyes, turn my head and open them again to look at her straight on. Finally she sighs, lifts her bag of peanuts above her head and lets a stream of them drop into her mouth. Then she wipes a bunch of salt off the cover of her log book.

Her black sweater's crept up on her shoulders
again, making her look all hunchback. I can't stand
that. I sit up straight and arch my back, listen to my
vertebrae snap at the back of my neck.

"I wish it was tomorrow already," I say. "I don't
think I can stand the rest of Wednesday."

"You could wish for anything in the universe and
all you want is for it not to be Wednesday anymore."

"Yeah, well, it's better than wishing to visit the
Andromeda Galaxy. Tomorrow it will no longer be
Wednesday and we'll be sitting here with my dream
having come true and yours still circling overhead ten
trillion light years away."

"It's only 2.3 million light years away. Don't bore
me with inaccuracies, Squeak."

She swore she wouldn't call me that. I throw down
my meatloaf sandwich. The kaiser comes open and the
meat flops out onto the table. Goody raises her eyebrows, grabs my chocolate milk and slugs it back. I
rebuild the sandwich and get mustard all over my
fingers.

I bring these huge lunches and try to squeeze them
all down me but after a few bites everything begins to
taste like black licorice. I'm determined to get bigger,
so what I've been doing is taking bigger bites.

Goody saves her talk for when I'm chewing. She
says I'm more guaranteed to listen that way. She flips

open her log book to the last printed page, looks at it and sighs.

"I set the alarm to catch Venus rise this morning, but it was cloudy. I hate that. First thing I have enough money, I'm heading for Arizona to lie in the desert and stare at the sky."

"And search the cosmos for large objects like Planet Goody Pryne," says Josie. She's trying to squeeze behind Goody's chair. Josie's short friend, Tsula, is moving toward their regular table from the other direction. Josie obviously took this route just for the joy of picking a fight with Goody. And Goody looks downright happy to see her. I swear – for those two, a day without a fight is like a day without sunshine.

I shrink back in my chair and touch the edge of my dad's wallet through my back pocket. I have one of my swatches in there. It helps.

"Look, Stevie, Josie's splurging on fries today. Go easy on the ketchup, Josie. I hear it tastes way better going down than it does coming up."

Josie puts her tray on the table and turns to Goody with her hands on her hips. Her hair's pulled back in one of those super-tight ponytails that makes it look like it's holding a girl's face on. She's so tough in the face with her bony cheeks and mean, pointy eyebrows. Her brown skin has this green tinge to it. She looks like an under-ripe baby potato.

"You should know. You're the expert on French fries. Your disgusting lard ass is made of them. No wonder your mother can't stand the sight of you. I bet she bursts into tears just looking at her ball of blubber daughter. Blubber, blubber, boo-hoo. Poor Mother Pryne left alone in her broken home with giganti-kid."

Josie usually sticks strictly to the fat jokes. Bringing Goody's mom into this is like juggling dynamite. I can tell Goody is biting the inside of her lip to keep from reacting too strongly. I shrink lower in my chair and dig my nails into my legs.

"Better shut your mouth, Josie," she says, loud enough that heads turn toward us. "You wouldn't want to accidentally swallow anything. You might develop substance."

Josie looks happy. She knows she got Goody good. She actually smiles, but then her face goes hard as a slab of solid steel as she leans in for the kill.

"I know you make your father sick. That's why he doesn't come around except on blue moons. 'Oh, no, look, a blue moon. Gotta go visit my gag-reflex.'" Josie clutches her non-existent stomach and wretches four inches from Goody's face. A look passes between them that seems familiar, almost friendly.

Josie just fake-puked over the line. Never tease Goody about her dad. Never.

"Quiet, Expletive," says Goody, standing up to

push her bulk against Josie's skeletal body. I swallow. The wad of sandwich wedged in my throat becomes a painful ball of leaking licorice.

"Let's go to the library," I say softly. I've never even tried to break them up before. She's got to know things are bad for me to get in the middle of this.

But Goody just pushes herself closer into Josie. Josie's snapping white teeth bite the air in front of her. I can't look at them.

Bea Fong is looking at Goody with half a sandwich poised in her hand. She chews slowly and gently, as if she doesn't want to hurt the food. She wipes the crumbs off her fingers between bites.

I can't stand how truly beautiful Bea is. I can't stand to watch her watch me be part of this. The cafeteria lady comes out from behind the cash register to break up Josie and Goody.

I turn into the main aisle of the caf two seconds before the cafeteria lady gets to the table. I beeline it for the door, keeping that picture of Bea chewing right in the front of my mind.

When I get to the library, I stick around in the open space by the door so that I can see Goody's face when she walks in and know how to act with her. I end up standing at the big podium with the dictionary on it. I look up the word pudding: 1. a soft cooked food, usually sweet. 2. a kind of sausage. 3. anything soft like a pudding. 4. a silky smooth white spread that perfectly compliments the ivory skin of Bea Fong's inner arm.

"What are you looking up?" Goody asks behind me. I look at the dictionary page.

"Pugnacious," I say.

"Oooh. Describes those who enjoy fighting. That's a good one, Stevie. You're absolutely right about that." She automatically assumes that what I'm doing is something to do with her. I look at the definition.

"That's what you are, one hundred percent," I confirm.

"I'd say it applies twenty-five percent. You don't know me half as well as you think."

"Okay, fifty percent then, 'cause I know you at least twice as well as you think I do."

We go and sit down. I reread the depression section of the psychology book for the millionth time. I keep one of my swatches in there. Goody doesn't know. She reads yet another book by this local astronomer, Terence Dickinson.

Goody convinced my mom to drive up to Yarker for a tour of his observatory once. The thing was like a garage with a roll-off roof. It was cloudy that night, but we still stood in line to look through the telescope. Mom and Goody saw clouds. When I got there, though, the moon poked through for a few seconds and I got to see the mountains on it. Goody was so jealous, she was mean to me for three days.

Chapter 4

Max Revy picks on me because I looked at
him the wrong way in grade eight. I saw him
in the schoolyard waving in my direction, and
I looked behind me to see who he was waving
at. When I looked back, he had this puzzled look on
his face. I couldn't figure out what was going on, so I
just kept on moving. There must have been something
wrong with my eyes when I looked back at him,
though, because he's been out to get me ever since.

It's occurred to me since then that maybe he was
waving at me that day.

Max Revy kicks at the back of my chair during
French class, jamming me farther and farther into my
desk and making a lot of noise. I can feel the tread of
his $150 platform Nikes right through my chest.
Everyone ignores it, including me, until I can hardly
breathe, he's got me shoved in so far. I put up my hand
to ask Mrs. Dorosh to get him to stop and she makes
me say it in French.

"Arretez, s'il vous plaît," I say. My voice goes from deep to foghorn as I talk.

"I don't plaît," Max says, and everyone laughs. Even Goody, who looks up from her log book to do it.

I quickly gather my stuff and move to an empty desk at the back of the room and that shuts them up.

I shoot Goody the evil eye, but I'm sitting behind her so it's completely ineffective.

I try to look angry after school and only grunt while she stands by my locker yapping at me about how she needs a new winter coat. Then I don't talk to her the whole way to The Store Famous. I'm waiting for her to notice that I'm not talking to her, but she's chewing on her lard lips like she's got something else on her mind.

When we get there, I don't even bother to pretend to be looking for anything. I just hang at the cash, waiting for Goody to nab us some snacks. Kent stares at me. I cross my hands across my chest so he can't accuse me of anything. Goody finally comes up to the cash and takes a couple of sour face pulls from the jar beside the counter, tells me to pay Kent and swings out the door.

"You going to pay for that juice, too?" he says.

"I didn't see a juice."

"$1.89," he says, so I know he's including the juice. I exhale loudly and give him the money.

"You owe me $1.40," I tell Goody when I get outside. "He saw you take the juice."

"So? Add it to my bill," she says. "What am I up to?"

I unzip Dad's wallet, noisily flip through the patched-up pictures of my father and pull out Goody's bill. At the bottom I write, "Juice $1.40," and add it in. "That's $69.84. As if you're ever going to pay it." I tuck the piece of paper back in front of the emergency swatch I've got stashed there.

"You could always donate my debt to the Arizona fund," she says.

"No, I want it. I want you to owe it to me because you owe it to me."

"I think it should even out with the stuff I've stolen for you over the last couple of years. I probably stole more than I owe."

"Yeah, but I didn't ask you to do that."

"No, but you expect me to do it." She shoves a hand into her windbreaker and pulls out a bag of all-dressed chips. "Here." I flip the pack out of her hand and we both watch it bounce on the yellow line on Barrie Street.

"Maybe I don't want it this time," I say. She picks up the pack of chips and crunches it against my stomach.

"You do too want it. So take it and shut up," she

says. I still don't take it. I hold my arms stiff at my sides. I do want the chips, but I swear, she always gets her way.

When it becomes obvious that we aren't moving until I take the chips, I grab the bag from her and rip it open, letting half of them fall on the road. Goody raises her eyebrows.

We're heading for the swings in Skeleton Park. It was Halloween last week and an orange streamer hangs off the bar that holds the swings. I sit on one of them and feel the cool chains squeeze in against my sides. I take a huge handful of chips and cram them in my mouth.

"You shouldn't have laughed at me in French today," I say.

"I'm sorry," she says right off, like I'm the one who's been making her wait to talk about it. She pulls my swing toward her and I'm caught in Planet Goody Pryne's gravitational pull. I put my foot out and push her swing away and drag my feet through the sand. I chew chips and steal a look at Goody.

"Are they officially divorced yet?" I ask, knowing the question will bug her. She shakes her head and slumps down in her swing like a giant stuffed animal. Her frizzy hair hangs in front of her face. I can just make out that she's chewing her lip.

I rock wide and catch the side of the swing frame.

I look over at Goody. She looks so innocent now, but I can still hear the echo of her laughing at me in French class.

I let go of the pole so that I slam into her sideways. I hear an "oof" and she falls out of the swing flat on her back.

"Are you okay?" She can't catch her breath. Maybe she punctured a lung. I hold my swing still and look back, silently begging her to breathe soon. When she opens her mouth she starts laughing.

When Goody laughs you almost want to put your hand over her mouth to get her to stop. When she takes a breath, it feels like she could swallow the whole world by accident. I hold my hand out to help her up. She yanks herself up into a low bend and gasps in my face so that I can see bits of the sour face pulls in her teeth and her pouffy hair scrapes my chin.

"HA. HA. HA." Hoover. "HA. HA."

Once she's done being loud at my nose, she staggers forward and keeps on going, still bent. She starts walking out of the park. She has to be home by four-thirty because of her chores.

I scoop out the last handful of chips. It tastes like licorice.

"Fifty percent pugnacious, eh? That's pretty high," she yells at me.

"I'm not saying it's a bad thing," I yell back. She

gives me the peace sign and I watch her make her way out of the park.

You know you've got Goody thinking when she brings stuff up like that way after it happened. That's how you always get Goody thinking, though. It has to be by accident.

When I go downstairs to check on dinner, Mom's on the phone with Aunt Lorraine. There's a casserole in the oven and carrots boiling on the stove. I hear them knocking against the side of the pot, with the top rattling like there's a trapped animal in there. I start setting the table with one eye on the pot.

I would go over to Goody's after school so that we could hang out more, but her place has bad vibes. First of all, it's a very clean house. Like, if I dropped sugar on the floor there, I'd get on my knees and lick it up because I'd be afraid of dirtying one of their dish cloths. Also, no worries about germs on that floor. It's quiet, too, because they never have the TV on. Mrs. Pryne reads in bed all the time. That woman creeps me out.

The last time I went over there, me and Goody sat on the picnic table in the back yard. Goody was pointing out constellations to me even though it was still daylight. She pointed at the empty sky and called out names. I said I couldn't quite make them out and so she drew them in the log book, which is just pages and pages of dots that don't mean anything to anyone except Goody. She knows the whole sky so well that she can draw it from memory. To me they just looked like pencil marks, but to her…it was almost like she was making the star when she put it on the page.

Anyway, we were laughing because it was so sunny out that every time we looked up we got spots in our eyes, and then I noticed Mrs. Pryne at the kitchen window. She was standing there watching us. She's a tall, skinny woman. She keeps her frizzy hair in a braid and has those square rimless glasses that politicians wear. She works at the registrar's office at Queen's University and she still had her suit on when she was watching us. Even when she saw that I saw her, she kept staring. I'd been looking over Goody's shoulder at her log book, and I moved away from her.

"What?" Goody said, giggling, and then she looked up. Her mom was still staring at us. She didn't move or smile or do anything but stand and look.

Goody closed the log book and said, "I have to go." Then she walked to the house. Her mother didn't take her eyes off me, though. She looked at me so hard, I thought maybe something was behind me so I looked over my shoulder. When I looked back Mrs. Pryne was gone and Goody was sweeping the kitchen floor.

"What the hell are you doing, Stevie?" Mom hollers from across the room.

I look down at the table. I've set three places and even put Dad's cup out.

I close my eyes and pray to get sucked into another dimension, but when I open them again I'm still in the kitchen and Mom's still standing there with yell in her eyes and Dad's still never coming back.

Chapter 5

Next morning, it's one of those gray-sky days where it's like the sun is shining through a piece of paper. Goody's waiting for me on the swings at Skeleton Park.

"I've been thinking about what happened yesterday," she says.

"Uh-oh, what'd I say?" I back away from her.

"Don't be like that," she says and stands up.

"I thought we decided that being a weeny sucky weasel was my job."

She takes a breath and holds it. She looks hurt.

"You aren't supposed to be scared of me, though," she says. I stand still, waiting. "I was talking about what went down between me and Josie." She stares at me a moment like she's going to tell me something and then changes her mind. She starts walking out of the park. I have to run to catch up with her.

"Just tell me what happened with you two," I say. "Maybe I can help."

Goody looks at me and shakes her head, biting her lip. She was maybe going to tell me, but now she's not. Case closed. The portal to that secret only opens once every few months, and I slammed it shut with a bad joke.

My inner black hole lengthens into a sliver and jabs at the back of my throat.

We have a test in geography that I forgot about.

I like tests. I like how quiet it is in the room and the sounds of pens scratching on paper. A test isn't just a test of what you know. It's a test of your method. Like, if you are Max Revy and you spend most of your class time figuring out ways to torture Man Child Stevie Walters or trying to get pens to stand on end on your palm, then in all likelihood you are going to flunk your geography test.

I have a different method. It's simple. It's called Listen in Class.

I finish the test early, put my head down on my desk and stare out the window at the last leaves blowing off the big maple tree across the street.

My mind drifts back to Goody and Josie at lunch yesterday. Usually when they start in on each other I just clench my jaw and wait for it to be over, like Mom does when we're stuck in Gardiners Road traffic.

Goody and Josie and Max – they're like my traffic and, I swear, I always have to be on the lookout for how they're moving around me.

I'm tired of feeling like a squirrel on the freeway. But it never occurred to me until this morning to try to clear the road.

My mind flashes back to Goody's face the second before she was going to tell me the secret of why she and Josie fight. She wanted to. If only she would tell me, maybe we could figure something out so at least it wouldn't get as bad as yesterday.

Like that could happen. Like my life could change. I'm doomed to watch and wait with my head on this desk while Bea Fong graduates high school, goes to university, gets a job as a lab technician, meets a dental surgeon, gets married, has children, learns yoga and grows her hair longer and longer and blacker and blacker and buys high-heeled shiny red shoes with bows on the top and a short, tight gold dress...

The bell goes but I don't move.

"Are you coming?" asks Goody. "I'm going to the library." I don't feel like getting up when my mental picture of Bea Fong is so strong and delicious.

"As soon as I leave this classroom, something bad is going to happen. I can feel it. Can't I just sit here?"

I flip my head on the desk so I can see Goody's face. She looks so tall from this angle, and I can see the underside of her chin. "I don't have to do what you say."

"Yes, you do," she says. I blink. She doesn't. I flip my head on the desk again.

"I'm staying here."

"Fine." I can hear her shoes grunt down the hall. I close my eyes again, but the image of Bea Fong is gone. I sit up and look out the classroom window. It's already beginning to get a little darker outside. I can see my reflection looking back at me. My hair's all spiky and shaggy. My head is triangular. It's all big at the top and then points down into my scrawny neck. My shoulders look spindly and weak. I've been wearing these jeans since grade six.

What I can't make out in my window reflection are my eyes. What I can make out is the ghost of Max Revy standing in the doorway, his shoulders hunched into his short pimply neck, eyeing me like a vulture.

I sigh deeply, pick up my books, walk to the door and stand there with my head down, hold up a peace sign and wait for Max to punch me in the shoulder, which he does.

☆ ☆☆◇ ☆ ☆ ◇☆☆
       ☆ ☆☆

I meet Goody coming out of the library. She's got a book about Muhammad Ali tucked under her arm.

"That's what you wanted to look up?"

"Yeah, Expletive. Got a problem?" She walks straight past me and pushes through the hall door with her stomach. Goody's a good six inches taller than me and at least eighty pounds heavier. I fall in behind her. I can tell from the stiff movement of the wrinkles on her back that I'd just better keep quiet.

We head out the front doors. The sun's already sinking, giving the sky that eerie blue glow that makes me feel like I'm walking in the stratosphere, some-where above the clouds, away from everything and everybody. I pick a spot behind Goody's elbow and stick to it as we make our way home.

It's kind of peaceful with Goody when she's too huffed up to talk. I listen to the crows. I listen to rock radio float through an open window right beside the sidewalk. I look through the window at a kitchen table and see some guy's hairy arm, a cup of coffee and an ashtray.

Then Goody steps on a stick and it breaks the mood. She looks at me like a bull dog eyeing a kitten.

"Josie wants to fight me? Fine, she can put up her dukes and show me what she's got, put her money where her mouth is. I'll beat her fair and square with my two fists. I'll punch in her big mouth, make it so she won't dare say one thing to me again for the rest of her sorry life."

"What are you talking about?" I ask.

"This is what I'm talking about," she says, showing me her fist. "This seems to be the only language Josie really understands." Goody knocks her fist into her hand so hard that the snap of it echoes down the street.

"That must have hurt," I say, testing.

"Careful, Stevie. I'm in the mood to annihilate something, so something better stay out of my way."

She forges ahead of me, her hands in fists, looking for something to hit. But there's nothing but cars and trees and hydro poles out here on the street.

Except me. I hang back and try to stay out of her line of sight as we continue down York Street.

I feel a twitch at the base of my spine. I have to talk Goody out of this. Only, because it's Goody, I've got to say the exact right thing or it will turn out even worse than if I didn't say anything.

Three blocks of silence later we come up on The Store Famous and I go to turn in, but Goody walks on by toward the park. I can see Kent through the window.

"You're not going to the store?"

"God, you'd think you were hot for Kent instead of Bea."

"Like you're hot for Josie," I say, hoping she'll laugh and the whole thing will be over.

"I'm totally serious, Stevie. I'm not taking this crap

for a whole other year," she seethes. I wait for lightning to come out of the top of her head. I wrack my brain for the one right thing I can say that will defuse Goody. I accidentally make eye contact with her. She looks like she might cry. I reach out to pat her on the arm.

Then she socks me in the stomach so hard I can't breathe. I double over in agony and catch a close-up look of Goody's worn sneakers. She keeps the laces undone. She's got a ring of dirt round her socks right where her leg meets her foot.

My lungs open briefly and I gulp down some air.

"See? I knew I had it in me. It's your own fault, you know, Stevie. You were the one who put it in my head that I was a pugilist. I didn't break any ribs, did I?"

When she leans over to check my face, that crying look is gone from her eyes.

She hit me because she couldn't stand to see me be sorry for her. So she's right. It is my own fault. I should know that by now.

Her palm knocks gently against my back. "You okay, Stevie? Come on, stand up."

I drop one hand from my stomach and try to stand up, but it hurts so I fold over again. Goody leads my bent body across the street to the park and pulls me toward a bench. She wipes the leaves off the seat and pushes me to sit down. I feel her arm come over my back. Again my lungs open and I gasp. It's like something's unlocked a bit and I can breathe a bit better.

My head's ringing. Goody's rubbing my back, but it's like it's happening in another universe. Goody told me once that scientists think that there may be many universes. I couldn't truly picture it until now with my lungs in one universe and my back in another.

"So you get why this has to be a formal fight, right, Stevie? I can't just hit somebody out of the blue like that. It's not fair. I want this to be a fair fight. Josie can take her best shot at me. I want her to. Here, hit me." She stands up in front of me and opens her arms to the sky. I shake my head and rub my stomach.

I'm trying to make sense of what she's on about in her universe, but I'm all foggy. A fair fight with bony Josie Bissell? She took me out with one punch.

"Come on, Expletive. You aren't going to let me get away with socking you one like that and then not hit back?"

I shake my head again. I try to sit up and it works a little bit. My ears have cleared up. I hear the wind running over the sand in the playground.

"Stevie. You gotta hit me. You can't let me go home like this. It's not fair."

I fall back against the bench and my shoulder knocks into it right where Max Revy hit me.

All I want to do is get home. I stagger up and start down the path.

"Stevie," Goody yells after me. "You knocked me out of the swing yesterday, remember? We're even."

I don't stop. I'm too tired. I want to go home and sleep for forty years. Probably Bea and Kent will have gotten divorced by then, and maybe I'll have finally had my growth spurt.

"You're hurting my feelings, Stevie," she yells, and I can hear that vibe in her voice that scares me. The one that wobbles like a plane just before it falls out of the sky. I half want to turn back, but I don't have the energy.

Besides, I don't want her to feel better.

When I get to the corner of the park, I look back. She's gone.

Chapter 6

Ten o'clock Thursday night. Physical status: sore stomach, sore shoulder, leaking licorice throat, exhaustion. I'm lying on the couch with a cushion between my knees and another hugged to my chest. Mom's asleep in her green recliner with a *National Geographic* bent over her stomach. It was Dad's subscription. Mom can never keep her eyes open pretending to read it.

The light from the television flickers on her face. I've been watching a show, but I couldn't tell you which one because really my mind is on kickboxing Kent and winning Bea Fong. Only, in my mental kickboxing ring, we fight in jeans and T-shirts. I mentally kick Kent in the head and he falls to the canvas and bounces off it, his arms flopping at his sides like wet noodles. Then I mentally look over at Bea, and she only has eyes for me and my sweaty T-shirt.

I'm not insane. I know she'd never really fall for me.

At the next commercial I go upstairs. I peel my shirt off and search my chest for signs of growth. I can see only bones rippling under my skin. I'm purple where Goody socked me.

I knew she was in a mood. I should have been more careful. She's so crazy when it comes to Josie. I mean, look at my stomach. One Goody punch did this.

I press the edges of the bruise and suck in when the pain hits. I take the small square mirror from the top of my bureau, wipe the dust off it on my leg and use it to try to see my back. I can see where the ribs curve from the back to the front of my body. I lift my arm and look at the pathetic tuft of hair there, hanging like a piece of seaweed out of the deep hollow of my armpit.

Is this what I'm always going to look like? Am I going to be walking around forty years old and still small, with a small man's face and a small man's body in some small suit that never wears out?

The phone rings. I listen and wait. Must be Aunt Lorraine.

I turn on the radio. I turn it way up so I can feel the music vibrate through my legs. It's the Tragically Hip. I let the guitar riffs control my arms, the voice gets my head, on comes the chorus and I can't help where my feet are going. I close my eyes. I feel the beat knocking in my heart and filling my head. I sing into my fist with everything I've got. The music's like a car without brakes careening down a mountain so fast it's like Niagara Falls and I'm right there with it, pounding my foot against the floor like I'm trying to stomp out everything. Stomp. It. All. Owowowowowoouuut.

Gone. The music's gone. I open one eye and there's Mom standing beside the stereo with her hand on the volume knob. I drop my fist microphone from my mouth.

"Sorry," I say. I stand waiting for the fall-out, for her to burn or melt, or for me to get it. She just stands there looking at my stomach with those sleepy eyes of hers.

"Put your shirt on. I'm taking you down to Emergency," she says. "That was Goody on the phone. She was worried about how hard she hit you today and I can see she did a job. Now, come on, so it won't take all night."

"Mom, we don't have to go. I'm all right. I swear." Goddamn, Goody. Why can't she live one night with me being angry at her? "Mom."

"No, Stevie. You come now. We're going. I don't know why you don't tell me about these things. Do you really think I'd let you go to bed with broken ribs? It's a good thing your girlfriend has some sense."

"She is not my girlfriend, Mom."

"Get your shoes on and get in the car."

We don't talk on the way there. I know what it means for her to take me down to the hospital. It's where they took Dad, even though they knew he was dead already. They'd already found the licorice in his mouth and caught the driver from the bowling alley and all that was left was for Mom to confirm that Dad was who he was.

I came down with her. The policeman met us at the door. He looked at me like I was a little kid. I mean, young. I knew looking young would save me from having to go in with Mom and I was glad. I didn't want to see Dad dead. I saw him dead later at the funeral, but that was after they fixed him up a bit. Mom had to go through those hospital doors alone. She went in and came out. It took maybe seven seconds altogether.

She looked at me and nodded her head and we haven't been able to look at each other since. Not really. Now Mom only looks at me when she's angry. Like the time she found out I skipped school and went to the movies. She sat me down at the kitchen table, told me that the school had called and that she knew what I'd done. Then she watched my eyes as she ripped up a picture of Dad in front of me.

"You think he's not around to see you go wrong? You think you can do what you want now? I'm telling you I'm not going to stand for it. I've got enough to take care of without you misbehaving. He's not here to take care of you or me anymore so we've got to take care of ourselves. You see this, Stevie? Let this be a reminder to you to take care." She pushed the pile of torn pieces of Dad toward me and left the table.

I taped the picture back together and put it in his wallet. I've got three pictures of him Scotch-taped together like that. I feel the edges of the wallet as we head into the Emergency Room. Mom sits down straight away like it was all she could do to get me here. I go up to the desk and wait for the nurse to look at me.

Then I see Tsula, Josie's go-to girl, sitting on the other side of the door. She looks away when I see her. She's sitting beside some guy, probably her brother. His hand's wrapped in a dish towel and he's holding it up in the air. I turn my back to her and wait for the nurse who is taking forever on the phone. Isn't this supposed to be the Emergency Room? I look over and Tsula's got this sarcastic smile on her face.

"What's so funny?" I say to her. No use pretending like we don't see each other when we're the only ones in the room.

"Nothing," she says. I notice a Tupperware container on her lap.

"Did your mom make you sandwiches for the trip?" I say.

"Show him," her brother says.

"I'm not going to show him," she says and holds the container closer to her body. Then the nurse is off the phone. I explain the situation of being punched in the stomach and she looks over at my mother. I tell her it was a friend that did it when we were play-fighting and my mom made me come down even though there's nothing wrong with me. She gives me some forms to fill in to get a hospital card.

Mom goes out to get some air and I'm tired of waiting way before Tsula comes over and says, "You want to see?"

She's got the Tupperware container with her. Before I have a chance to say no, she whips off the top and there, nestled in a bed of ice, is a tubular slice of white skin. I wait for myself to freak out like the weeny sucky weasel that I am, but it all happens so fast that I don't really have time to get worked up.

"Which finger?" I ask.

"Index. He was cutting a bagel. Mom made me come down with him in a cab. What are you doing here?"

It's a dangerous question. I don't know what to say so I roll up my shirt. Tsula's eyes open wide.

"What happened?"

I look around, as if Goody could materialize and belt me another one just for standing in the same orbit with Tsula. I'll bet she's lying in her rubber raft on the picnic table trying to pick out Jupiter's moons – the four of them that you can see through binoculars.

I open my mouth to tell Tsula I don't know what, when the door swings open and in comes Mom.

"Who's this?" she asks, looking at Tsula.

"It's Tsula from school, Mom."

"Oh. Haven't they let you in yet?" I shake my head. "Have you even gone over there? You think I want to be here all night? Come on, Stevie, shake a leg. I'm aging by the minute." She sits down hard. Tsula sits beside her with the Tupperware still on her lap. I walk up to the counter and ask the nurse how long it will be.

"We'll get to you when we get to you," she says.

When I get back to Mom, Tsula's shaking the Tupperware container and is just about to open it when I jump forward to stop her hand. Her fingers are cool and smooth and they stay under my hand just one second longer than they need to. Then she yanks her hand back and puts it in the pocket of her ski vest.

"She asked to see it," Tsula says, looking up and straight at me with her gold eyes, and it's like she's frozen me so that I can't look away from her face or stop from noticing how her short dark-chocolate hair brushes the edge of her chin beneath her round cheeks. She has turned me to ice.

I can't turn my head. I can't blink. The world is hard static until she turns those eyes off.

The voice of the nurse penetrates the static and suddenly the chair in front of me is empty. I prop my hands on its arms and lower myself into it sideways. Tsula and her brother converge at the front desk. She turns before they go into the examining room.

"I hate you," she mouths at me. Then she goes.

Mom's looking at me.

"What?" I say.

"Is she why Goody hit you?"

"I told you, me and Goody are just friends. I don't know why you won't believe me. Besides, I could never like Tsula."

"Why not?"

"Because I like – " I almost spill it, but catch myself at the last moment. Mom wouldn't understand about Bea Fong's arms. I don't want her to understand.

"Because you like Goody," she goes on.

"It's not that. I promise you, that's not it." The nurse calls me. "Finally," I say and nearly run to her.

The doctor who sees me looks like an eighteen-year-old video-game junkie. He has huge rings under his eyes. He gets me to lift my shirt.

"You didn't need to come down here, you know," he tells me. He pokes around my stomach, which hurts like hell, then says I'm perfectly fine. He starts going on about people coming down to Emergency for every little ache and pain and I phase out. I can see Tsula's red sneakers beneath the curtain around the next bed. I watch the feet turn so that the toes are pointing toward me. Her sneakers are all cracked around the toes. I can see her socks straight through them.

It's funny how you don't usually think of people as having feet. Why did Tsula have to have feet?

I pop off the bed and walk past muttering Dr. Burn-out and head straight through to the waiting room.

"I'm all right. Let's get out of here."

Chapter 7

"'No person is to hit his adversary when he is down, or seize him by the ham, the breeches, or any part below the waist: a man on his knees is to be reckoned down.' Those are the Broughton Rules of 1743. I looked it up on the Internet," says Goody. I'm walking beside her, but it doesn't mean I've let her off the hook for what happened yesterday.

I pull the piece of paper she's been reading out of her hand.

"'To Be Observed in All Battles on the Stage.' We weren't on stage yesterday. Seems like that's the top, main rule for making it all right to hit someone. They've got to be ready for it."

"You look like you'll live. This could work, Stevie. I get her in the ring, we fight and then it's all over," she says. I still haven't told her about seeing Tsula at the hospital. She pulls the paper with the list of rules back and folds it carefully. I can see what it is to her.

It's like a permission slip to kill Josie and get away with it.

"What makes you think Josie's going to go for it? It's one thing to snap at each other like turtles over lunch. It's something else to get her to box."

"Like turtles, Stevie? Nobody fights like a turtle, you freaky little idiot."

"You know what I mean. You can ask her, but there's no guarantee she'll do it."

Goody just shrugs.

"You don't ask someone to have a fight with you, Expletive. You challenge them. I look forward to the day that I get to grind that girl's face into peanut butter."

"Why not just do it then? You could flatten her in two seconds." Goody stops in her tracks and turns to me. Tufts of blonde frame her face like a lion's mane.

"Because. I want it to be our last fight. And for it to be our last fight she has to agree to the rules, Stevie. I want her to see my fist coming at her face and know that she agreed to let me smash her hideous pin head. That's what the rules are for. They take the blame off the fighters. The stupid rules keep it fair, clean and right and show you how to end it. Me and Josie could go at it in the cafeteria every day forever. At least in the boxing ring, there's a real end to the fight. Isn't that what you want?"

She looks at me to see if I'm buying what she's selling. I nod slowly, trying hard to believe she wants this to end as much as I do.

"Don't worry," Goody says, looking away. "Josie will do it. She'll think the rules will make it safe to hit me."

I do want the fight to be over. I just don't want it to be over Josie's dead body. Leave it to Goody to come up with a legal form of murder.

Lunchtime. Cafeteria. Max left me alone all morning. I know it's because Goody is rolling around the school in a spiky steel bubble of rage. Even I'm afraid of her. Only it's different for me because it would be more dangerous for me not to hang out with her. It's like if I go too far away from her, I'll walk through some hidden force field that triggers the mechanism that sets her off.

How would you like to have a bomb for your best friend?

At least Goody hasn't said anything more about boxing Josie, which might mean she's having second thoughts.

She's got two plates of fries in front of her. I can almost taste them. I put my sandwich down on my paper bag and watch it turn into a huge chunk of licorice. I didn't even get two bites in.

"I wish we were transferable," I say.

"You mean you wish you could be somebody else? Like Kent?"

"No, I mean I wish you could take part of you and put it on me."

She stares at me like I've got her stumped. Then she grabs my sandwich and takes a huge bite, closing her eyes. When she opens them, she licks her finger and smiles.

"Aw, that's real sweet, Pluto, but you know we're just friends, right?" I'm about to set her straight when I see Bea and Kent walking down the aisle holding hands, and I'm instantly pissed that not even my best friend thinks I'm worthy of being her boyfriend. Not that I want to be her boyfriend. But. Still.

"Pluto – smallest planet in the solar system?"

"Not even a planet," she points out.

I grab my sandwich out of her hand and sink my teeth into pure licorice. It leaks into my saliva and slips down my throat, burning me all the way down to my stomach.

"It's still on the map, though, Stevie. I mean, Pluto figures in the count. It's small, but it's got a name and everything. Someday, somebody could land on it. I think it's a good nickname for you. Beats Squeak."

"Planet Pryne," I shoot back. Her eyes flash and I feel better.

Josie circles around the back end of the caf with Tsula at her side. Tsula's got both hands in the pockets of her red and blue ski vest. I picture her hidden hand fiddling with the disembodied tip of her brother's finger, like it's an eraser. She opens and closes her mouth when she chews her gum so that it's easy to imagine the smacking sound of it reaching all the way to where I'm sitting.

I check out Goody to make sure she didn't see me looking, only Tsula picks that exact moment to turn her head in our direction. She catches my eye and I'm caught again, tied to the end of the golden chain of light beaming straight on me. The edges of the ray are crisp.

"Hey." Goody calls me out of it. "What's she looking at you for?"

I cross my arms and sit back in my seat.

"Maybe she was looking at you," I say, but the look on her face doesn't change. "My mother doesn't need you calling her and making her worry about me. She took me down to Emergency last night and I got an earful from the doctor because there was nothing wrong with me. You know what it meant for her to take me down there? Don't do that again. Tsula saw us going into Emergency, that's all."

Goody takes it in, crams some fries in her mouth, chews and swallows.

"You mean I didn't break anything?" she says, disappointed.

I'm so glad tomorrow's Saturday. Goody will be out at her dad's and maybe she'll forget about this whole boxing thing.

Like she ever forgets anything.

Me and Goody became friends when we both begged off of swim class. I still had the excuse then that my dad had just died and none of the teachers had the heart to make me do anything I didn't want to do. I didn't even have to say anything to the gym teacher. I just went and sat in the pool bleachers and nobody said boo. Normal gym is humiliating enough without having to walk around in front of girls without a shirt on.

Goody told the teacher she had plantar's warts. The teacher didn't ask to see them.

The first swim class we ignored each other. I was ready to go on doing that, but Goody can't take being ignored for too long. She came up and sat in the bleacher in front of me. I was afraid of her because I heard that she had pushed the Lifestyle and Ethics teacher into the oven during a meal test.

"You think the teachers care, but they don't really. What's it to them if you flunk swimming? They still get paid," she said to me. I was all into being sulky then so I didn't say anything back. "You waste all your time worrying about making them happy and the truth is, they don't give a floating turd so long as you aren't in-their-face flunking. Takes the same amount of energy to write an F as an A. If your parents care, that's one thing. My parents don't care, not about gym. They'd know I was putting them on if I flunked anything else. What about you?"

I shrugged and went back to sticking my hands inside their opposite sleeves where I had a couple of my blue cloth swatches hidden. I was still carrying them around back then. I would hold my swatches in my palms and squish my fingers down on top of them, which made a swishing sound, actually. When Goody discovered it, she started calling me Squeak and it sort of caught on with everyone. If she'd listened better, they would have been calling me Swish.

"Your father died, right?" she said, staring into the blue of the pool. I nodded. "That's too bad. If you liked him, I mean. Did you like him? He didn't hit you or anything, or make you clean up his spit and stuff, right?" Her head faced straight out so that I couldn't see her eyes.

"No. He was good. I wish he didn't die."

"That's nice, Stevie. That's a nice thing to say about your father. Where do you think he is?"

"He's in the Cataraqui Cemetery."

"I don't mean his body, Expletive."

"I don't know." She looked back at me. And then came up and sat beside me. Her hair rustled against her plaid windbreaker, which she didn't take off that whole year.

"When I die, I'm going to the Andromeda Galaxy. If you get a choice, I mean. I hope we do... no, I really believe we do. I don't think we get given the whole universe and then don't get to see it, you know what I mean?"

I was staring down at the moving dots in the pool and listening to the echoes of the splashing and yelling coming off the walls, and my eyes blurred and sound zoomed in on itself so that I was swimming on the inside of my head, floating through a liquid pitch-black universe, slipping my hands through the sunshine of the stars. I opened my mouth and let the stars fall in, and the light tasted so sweet.

When I landed back in the bleachers, my swatches had fallen onto my feet and Goody was staring at me with that huge stunned grin she uses for the two minutes she's happy every month. I let the swatches slip off the tips of my shoes and squished them together with my feet.

"You are classifiable," she said.

"Plantar's warts, my ass."

It wasn't so much like we were friends at first. It was more that we just ended up in the same place all the time because of us both being too truly freaky for the other kids. I didn't so much like her as not mind her. She said interesting stuff. Then she began standing in front of me when Max was coming at me and she started walking home with me because she goes the same way and stealing me stuff from The Store Famous because she was hungry and I hate Kent. I don't like it when anybody else does stuff for me, but with Goody it's all right. She does it because she wants to, not because she feels like she has to because I'm pathetic and my dad's dead.

Anyway, that's how it started.

I probably wouldn't have ended up being a freak if my dad didn't die and Goody didn't become my friend. I think about that sometimes.

Crowfoot Library
Self Checkout

10:49 AM   2009/04/1

1. Aya of Yop City
39065100034154   Due: 5/9/2009,23:5

2. YA Paperback - Crow - 2006
39065088378045   Due: 5/9/2009,23:5

3. Deep/green : color me jealous [a novel]
39065093032082   Due: 5/9/2009,23:5

4. YA Paperback - Crow - 2006
39065088380728   Due: 5/9/2009,23:5

5. YA Paperback - Crow - 2006
39065088323223   Due: 5/9/2009,23:5

6. Young Adult Paperback - Crow - 2005
39065083811669   Due: 5/9/2009,23:5

7. YOUNG ADULT PAPERBACK - CROW - 2003
39065075145936   Due: 5/9/2009,23:5

Total 7 item(s).

To check your card and renew items
go to www.calgarypubliclibrary.com
or call 262-2928

Chapter 8

The library on Johnson Street has free videos. Most Saturdays, me and Mom go down to pick some out. It's a library, so there aren't any action flicks, but if it was ever a book, then they have the movie of it.

Today I thought I'd look for a boxing movie.

"Should have known I'd find you in the library, browner."

I turn around and there's Tsula.

"What are you doing here?"

"I'm with my brother. He keeps in touch with his girlfriend by e-mail, but we don't have a computer yet so he uses the ones here. He can't use his hand so I was supposed to type for him."

She moves around me and scans the videos. I look around to see if anybody is watching us.

"So why aren't you helping him?"

"He wanted to type something private. I bet she's sleeping around on him. I mean, she's already in university and he's washing floors at Taco Bell to save for a computer. Josie bet him twenty bucks that they'd be broken up before Christmas."

"That's not very far off."

"We'll see. Josie's hardly ever wrong." Tsula's put on some of that cream make-up over her zits. You can still see them underneath. I feel like reaching out and rubbing some of it off, like when you see food on somebody's chin.

Mom comes round from the other side of the rack.

"It's the girl from the hospital," she says, smiling.

"Hello, Mrs. Walters," Tsula says. Mom opens her mouth and I have this premonition that she's going to ask Tsula over. I grab a video off the shelf and shove it at Mom.

"What about this one?" I say too loudly.

"I'd better go see if my brother is done yet," Tsula says. I didn't mean for her to leave.

"Hey," I say to make her stop. But I don't know what to say. Both Tsula and Mom are looking at me, waiting for me to say something.

"Goody wants to box Josie," I blurt.

"She wants what?" Mom says.

"To box. You know, like Muhammad Ali." Stupid, stupid. What am I doing? Mom glares at me in disbelief.

"Are you serious?" Tsula asks. A hair falls into her

eye and she blows it out. "She is so disturbed. You should see her, Mrs. Walters. She's huge, and not just like fat, but big. Everyone's scared of her, except Stevie and Josie. I don't even like being in the same room as her. It's like being in a cell with an ax murderer – "

"All right, that's enough," Mom snaps. "I don't know what goes on with you kids at school, but for your information, I do know Goody. I know her very well. She is smart, funny, she's good to her mother and she looks out for Stevie. It's no wonder she comes off as a little cool in attitude if you kids are going around comparing her to an ax murderer."

Tsula looks shaken. I wish I'd let her go.

"She's entitled to her opinion," I say. Mom turns on me with flashing eyes.

"Goody's your friend, Steven."

Tsula's still standing there, waiting to be let out of this. She's going to be afraid to talk to me now. Not that she'll be able to, because Goody's going to kill me for telling her about the boxing idea. I scrunch into the space between the shelves and the wall. Mom takes a deep breath and softens a bit.

"You kids are so hard on anyone who's a bit different." I see Mom's arm reaching for me and I begin to die. Please, God, no. Her hand comes round my neck and onto my shoulder. Tsula's lower lip is sticking out.

Her eyes are hard against me. I can't stand it. I wriggle out of Mom's grip.

"I better go," Tsula says. I grab her by the sleeve.

"If you tell Josie about this, she'll know you were talking to me."

She jerks her arm out of my grasp and walks away.

I follow Mom through the library check-out line in a daze. When we get to the car, I look down at my lap and see the video we got: *Pride and Prejudice*.

"Am I going to have to call Goody's mom about this?" Mom says, touching my hair. Ever since she took me to Emergency she's gone weird. I jerk my head back.

"I don't think it's really going to happen," I tell her.

Mom's staring at me, looking at me like she hasn't since I can't remember when. I love how she only notices me when it's about Goody. I can tell she doesn't believe me.

"Goody's just mad because Josie got her good at lunch last week. You know Goody. Talking about boxing Josie is just her way of blowing off some steam. If she was actually going to go through with it, she would have challenged Josie already."

"Then why did you say that to that girl? You were trying to impress her, weren't you?"

Now that a girl's involved, she's interested in my life.

We're stopped at a red light. I sigh deeply and push my feet into the floor of the car.

"How could I like Tsula? She's Josie's best friend. You heard what she said about Goody. Besides, it's not exactly like I'm super-buff or anything."

"Goody likes you," Mom says. I nod my head stiffly and look out the window. On the corner, an old lady is trying to get her little black dog to put its paw in the armhole of a miniature tartan vest.

How can anybody do that to an innocent animal?

Chapter 9

Goody shuffles into math class late Monday morning wearing her black sweater. She rolls her eyes in my direction, slams her books on the desk and slumps down into her seat. A couple of guys in the next row inch their chairs away from her. I don't think they know they're doing it.

Goody's quiet at lunch. Too quiet. It's like she's wrapped in that yellow caution police tape. She hasn't said anything more about boxing Josie.

I put down my sandwich and examine Goody's face. She was going to let it go and I had to open my big mouth to Tsula. I look over to where Josie and Tsula are sitting. Tsula's lips are moving.

Why did I tell her?

Last week I was afraid Goody was going to kill Josie. Today I'm afraid she's going to kill me as soon as she finds out I spilled the beans to Tsula. My stomach shivers. I have to tell Goody what I did before she hears about it from Josie.

I take a deep breath and put one hand on Dad's wallet for strength.

"How was your dad's this weekend?" is what I manage to spit out. She picks up a French fry and twirls it in the air.

"Next subject," she mutters. I try to think of something to soften her up a bit. I rack my brain for some planet or nebula I could ask about, but it's hard to think with her staring at me with her razor eyes.

"What is it?" she asks. "Stop sitting there with your mouth half open. I can see the crud in your teeth. It's making me sick. Just say what you have to say."

Now I really can't talk. Goody crams in three fries, chews them up and opens her mouth to show them to me. I can't think.

"You're so pathetic when you're trying to outsmart me. I don't know why you bother."

"You have to tell Josie you want to fight her." There, I said something. I clear my throat again and watch Goody's head as it turns slowly and deliberately toward Josie's table and then shoots back to me.

"Why do I have to do that, Expletive?" She's squinting at me.

"You said you wanted it to be fair, but you've already got the advantage because you know you're going to fight her. Shouldn't she know so that she has a fair chance to prepare? Maybe she'll want to bulk up or something." Goody's face is getting red. I plunge on. "Look at her, Goody. If she were in the ring with a swan she might have a fighting chance, but my money'd be on the swan."

"This swan is fighting Josie because..."

"I don't know. I don't even really know why you want to fight her." She drops the fry in her hand back onto her plate and pushes the tray away. I'm careful not to change the expression on my face. Goody leans in.

"Chill out, Stevie. I'm not going to box her, all right? Don't look at me like that. You knew it was never going to happen. This whole thing has become so intensely boring, it just helped to picture smacking her around a bit," she says. I breathe out a sigh of relief. "Not like that would have solved anything anyway. How am I supposed end this, Stevie? Can you think of a way?"

"What about something with all your parents?"

"God! You are so way off," she snaps.

"What happened between you two? You know I won't tell." I watch the sides of her mouth stiffen. She wants to tell me but she can't.

Goody stands up. She looms over me, dressed in black like the shadow of death. I brace myself but she just moves past me. I catch her by the sleeve.

"What?" she says. I try to look her in the eye, but she won't let me. "I have to go to the washroom."

I let go of her elbow and watch her disappear through the doors. The cafeteria noise covers the sound of my hammering heart. The hockey guys at the next table stare at me.

I feel so exposed without Goody. It's like she's the bush I hide behind. I can't even look at Bea. I take one more bite and taste licorice.

"Get up," Goody says when she gets back. She tugs on my shoulder

"What?" I sputter.

"We're going to try diplomacy. We're going to open negotiations with Josie. Come on. Let's get this over with before I change my mind." She starts walking in that way she has that means business straight toward Josie and Tsula's table. I've got a feeling like I'm a cold can of cola all shook up. This is happening too fast.

When we get there, Tsula is sitting by herself reading. Goody makes straight for her and lifts up the cover of Tsula's book, which is some science fiction thing. Then she starts in on her.

"Very good, Tsula. Let me know when you get past page two. We'll discuss. Where is your prime exploiter?" Tsula looks up at her blankly. "Hello? This is not a trick question. I'm asking where Josie is?"

"She had a dentist appointment." Tsula looks at me.

No. Don't look at me. Goody'll know I said something. The fear comes on me and I shut my eyes.
When I open them Goody is looming over Tsula.

"If you see Skeletar, tell her I want to talk to her
about ending the war," Goody says.

"Don't you think the Big Bertha act is getting a little tired, Goody?" Tsula says. She still thinks Goody's
talking about a boxing match and looks at me to
confirm. I shake my head wildly, but she doesn't
understand.

The feet of Tsula's chair scrape noisily against the
floor of the cafeteria. The mental goes into Goody's
eyes as Tsula stands up to her. Goody takes a step into
Tsula and pins her against the chair with her chest.

"You are infinitesimal. You are inert. The shadow
of a dead cockroach has more power to affect me than
you do," she whispers loudly. She pushes into Tsula
who I can tell is scared but won't look away. "I'm bigger than Bertha will ever be, Tsula. I'm bigger than
anyone you'll ever know."

I feel eyes on us. I pull at Goody to get her off
Tsula. She pulls back fast and starts in the direction of
the caf line-up. I follow hard on her heels. She turns
on me, grabbing my arm. She pulls me past the line-
up, through the caf doors and into the back hall.
Bright afternoon sun streams in through the huge
windows that overlook the track. Outside I can see the

girls' rugby team warming up for their lunchtime practice. Goody lets go of my arm.

"What is going on with you and Tsula?" she says. The jig is now up.

"I told her you wanted to box Josie," I spill. As soon as it's out, I feel instantly better. Strong, even. I take a deep breath and feel my veins fill up. "I ran into her at the library on Saturday. She was there with her brother. It's not like we were on a date or anything."

"You wish..."

"She told me she hates me. I was just – "

"Wait. I'm having a hard time imagining this situation, where this girl who supposedly hates you, gets it out of you that I plan to challenge her best friend to a fight. If you were stupid, I'd understand it. Maybe she wagged her little butt and made you all stupid. Do you actually think she likes you? Could you possibly be that stunned?"

"I said she hates me." I feel like I'm on the verge of being sucked into oblivion.

"Yeah, and you sound all excited about it, too. Come on, Squeak. Think about it. A girl looks at you? A girl pays attention to you? I hate to break it to you, but it's not your body she's interested in, Man Child. She's working for Josie. She's working you."

She glowers at me and the space in front of my eyes blurs. I see Tsula's face flash in front of me. I see her mouth the words I hate you like she did in the Emergency Room. But the way I see it in my head, it's like she was saying she likes me. I can tell that's what Goody's thinking. She's thinking Tsula likes me.

She's pacing the empty hall, her hands on her hips.

"She could come in handy during diplomacy," I say.

Goody stops and laughs, throwing her head so far back it's like someone's pulling her hair from behind.

"You think I enjoy being in the middle of this?" I say to make her stop and she does, on a dime, and walks straight up to me and pokes me in the chest with her thick index finger.

"You love it, Stevie. Being in the middle of this is like chocolate milk over ice on a hot day in July. It's pouring all down you like 'ahhhh,'" she snaps.

I immediately feel liquid licorice burning like acid down my throat. I hate that she knows how to hit me. So many things Goody says hit right on the spot, exactly like chocolate milk over ice on a hot day in July. But that spot's all tender now. That spot's all black and blue.

I pinch my leg hard to keep myself from running away from her.

"Do you have any idea how much I hate you?" I hiss at her, and it chokes at the back of my throat.

"Get in line," she growls. We stand there stiff, staring at each other. The whites of her eyes are all murky and slimy, like wet mushrooms. I pinch myself harder and dare myself to look into the black middle of her irises. It's like I'm in one of those nightmares where you're in a dark basement and there's a low dark doorway at the end of the room and you just know whatever's behind it is sad and evil but you can't stop walking toward it.

I can't look anymore. I blink.

"Who's side are you on?" she demands. I take a deep breath and hold it. "Can I count on you or what?"

"Yes," I whisper.

Goody searches my face and lets me go. Her forehead smooths, her shoulders shrink down, she looks smaller. She's got huge rings under her eyes.

Big Bertha. That was a good one, but it's not quite right. That's not how Goody's big. There's more than a few kids in the school who outsize her. It's more like she's heavy, you know, intense. Goody's packed – like a neutron star. Four teaspoons worth of neutron star weighs about the same as the moon. A neutron star has a maximum density of material under maximum compression. That's Goody. That's Goody one hundred percent.

Chapter 10

Mom's talking with Aunt Lorraine about getting together at Christmas. I hate going to Belleville. Mom and Aunt Lori spend the whole time yapping in the kitchen and me and Uncle Burt just stare at each other in the living room. Sometimes he puts on a hockey game, which is a relief because then we don't have to talk.

Truth is, I don't really get hockey. Baseball's my game. Dad used to play on the company team and he'd take me down to mind the cooler. I got to sit with all the girlfriends and wives. One girlfriend used to sit right behind me and play with my hair. I didn't like it at the time, but I like thinking about it now. Another girlfriend would always pass me her beer when my dad went up to bat so that I could take a slug off it.

I don't want to go to Belleville without Dad. Actually, it was pretty much the same with Dad there – except that Dad was there.

I sit up on the couch, pull Dad's wallet out of my back pocket and fish through it for the little mirror he kept in there. Half the mirror stuff is worn off it, so I have to hold it away from my face in order to see both my eyes.

They're brown. Muddy like wet sand and squinty at the sides, like Dad's. Except his eyes were green. My eyebrows are like his, too. Short and straight, like two lines drawn to be the exact length of the eye. I stare at myself, like if I look hard enough I could see who I really am.

I fold the mirror back into Dad's wallet and go through the kitchen to go downstairs. Mom's still on the phone. I creep down to Dad's room, pull back the beaded curtain as quietly as possible and sit at his desk.

Fingerprints dot the dust on the desktop. They're smudgy Mom fingerprints, and a couple of spots that an arm might have wiped. I don't know why I thought she didn't come in here. I look at the shelves for the magazines and see that she's been adding to them. I listen for her and hear she's still on the phone. I crack the desk drawer open.

Inside is a pen from Dad's printing plant held together with an elastic band, some paperclips in a plastic box, a three-hole punch, an old address book, a calculator with the plant's logo on it, a take-out menu for the New Garden Chinese Restaurant and a framed certificate. I pull it out. It says: "Awarded to Roy Walters for 15 years of service." The plant logo is embossed in silver in the corner.

I've been in here twice since he died. I never took the certificate out before. I didn't want Mom to hear me. Not that she ever said not to come in here. I just knew she wouldn't like it. She was always angry when Dad was in this room. When Mom saw me going to sit on the basement stairs, she'd throw something in the sink like she was fed up with the both of us. I figured it was because she didn't like him to read down here instead of taking her out. Now, with her reading Dad's magazines, it's like she's trying to make it up to him.

I look back in the desk. There's a red binder under where the certificate was sitting. In a vinyl flap at the side are a bunch of forms and pamphlets. I pull one out. It's about a writing program in Toronto. The one behind it is about another one in Banff, and the one behind that is about one at St. Lawrence College. The rest of the binder is full of looseleaf paper. Most of it is unused, but the first eight pages are full. Half the stuff is scratched out, and you can tell from the ink that he used a different pen to go over the same bits several times.

It's a story – or parts of one. It doesn't seem to start at the beginning and there are comments on the side like, "Put with scene at waterfall."

I didn't know this.

I catch my name on the third page and start reading. *"We'll never make the lake alive, Captain. We've got to turn back now!" Steve implored. The captain placed his hand on the shoulder of the young sailor and peered deep into the navy pitch of the sky above the Congo. "No, Stevie. We must go forward. Fear will kill us harder than anything that lurks in the darkness ahead. Besides, we've got a date with the devil himself at that lake and it's a date I intend to keep." Steve couldn't think of anything else to say to the captain, but remained by his side nevertheless, quiet as a jaybird in despair.*

I flip through looking for more, but it's the only paragraph with my name in it. The captain's name is Wooster, though. That was the name of a dog Dad had when he was a kid. Actually, the dog's name was Woofster, named after his coughy, low bark. We have a couple of old photographs of him in the family album, a stubby black mutt with pointy ears and kinky hair. Now here he is captain of a river-boat expedition in Africa.

"What are you looking for?"

I look up through the beaded curtain and see Mom standing on the stairs. I swing around in the chair and knock my elbow against the desk, but I've still got a page between my fingers.

"Nothing. I was just here and I…didn't know Dad…"

Then I'm scared she might try to rip it up. I snap the binder shut and hold it across my chest. Through the lines of beads I see my mother make her way down the stairs. She wipes the dotted lines away with the back of her hand and looks around the room.

As strange as it is to be in here alone, it's that much worse with Mom here. It's like she just came in the men's room. She props her butt on the desk and flicks on the light switch by the door. The room's shadows disappear and a dust ray beams beneath the overhead light.

"You didn't like it when Dad came here," I say, still clutching the binder to my chest.

"No, you're wrong. I didn't like it when you came here." She looks at me and reaches out her hand. I try to dodge it, but it catches my head and brushes back my hair. She looks sad, but she smiles. "A man doesn't build an office for himself because he wants to read at a desk. I knew he wanted to write. I used to come down here before he got home and look in there to see what he'd done. You can see he never got far. So when I saw you coming down here, I thought maybe that's why he didn't go further."

"He was always reading. I never saw this before."

"I know. I think he liked it when you came down. I was jealous of the two of you if you want to know the truth. I wish he'd told me about wanting to write."

Her shoulders slump but the smile stays put. We sit there like that, her on the desk, me in the chair, looking around the room not saying anything.

I slowly let the binder drop to my knees. Mom moves her hand to my hair again and I push my head into it.

"We could make this into a study for you if you want," she says. I shake my head under her hand.

"Or you," I say.

"Nah, if I had an extra room it wouldn't be a study."

"What would it be?"

"I don't know," she says. I can tell she has an idea, though. She's thought of something without even wanting to. "Does Goody still have that Arizona fund going?"

"Yeah, but it doesn't have any money in it."

"You should have a fund like that," she says.

"You mean one with a zero balance?"

"No, one with a plan for something you want to do."

"I don't know what I want to do."

She stands up and goes back through the curtain toward the laundry room.

"You'll think of something," she says from the next room. She sounds so certain, but all I can think of is Goody telling me what a lousy wisher I am.

The next morning I watch balls of mist roll up the Bay Street hill and right into Skeleton Park. I've climbed the turtle-shaped mound of stones and mortar that marks the middle of the park's paths. I turn all ways, looking for Goody. The mist clings to my bare hands, making them feel like I've just washed them in lake water. I pull up the tab on my jacket to protect my neck. I turn toward Patrick Street.

No sign of her. Maybe she slept in again. Probably stayed up all night looking at the stars.

The corner of my eye catches the climbing set with the slide. I should really get my swatch out of there before winter comes. I climb down the rocks and make my way toward it. I'm halfway under the plat-form when I feel a tug at my back.

I am spun up against a tree. It's Josie. She's strong for a skinny girl.

"You meeting her here? I know you meet her here," she hisses in my face. Still stunned, I look down at the tight hold she has on the arm of my coat. I can see all of Josie's veins stretched to their limit, popping out of her scrawny arm. She's wearing a pink crocheted skull cap with her hair in a thin braid poking out the back. Her tiny bird neck makes her head seem to pop off her shoulders like one of those nodding dolls.

"I'm waiting for her, but I don't know if she's coming," I say. Josie grinds her teeth and pushes me deeper into the crust of the tree. I can feel the bark's ridges dig into my back. I look into the face of my best friend's enemy and watch her bones move where her jaw meets her head.

"That horse? She's probably at home fixing breakie for poor Mommy and secretly stuffing her own face with Ding Dongs and Hot Tamales. Or maybe she's busy plotting the galaxy in her little log book? Stardate: who gives a crap." Her eyes are scaring me. They're worse than angry. It's like they've got plastic wrap on them.

"Okay, I'll talk to her highness," Josie says. "But we'll do it here. Tell her. Tonight at five."

"Why don't you tell her?" I say, gathering up my knapsack.

"No. You tell her." She points at me and then opens her hand and pats the air between us. "I would have told her if she showed up. But there's no way I'm spending all day following her around like a weeny sucky weasel. Here at five. You can do that, right? You're the smart one, right?"

I nod.

Then she steps toward me and I feel the breath of the tiger on my neck. She's going for my jugular. It should end quickly. It will only hurt for one second and then it'll be over. I can almost see the line where the tiger's chin fades into Josie's mouth, like the horizontal hold on the TV set. I try to track it and it makes me dizzy. I clutch at the tree.

"What's the matter with you?" I hear her say. I push my hand in front of me to ward her off. I step away from the trunk and shake my head. When I'm steady enough to look up, she's gone. I pull myself together and start for school.

That weeny sucky weasel thing. I wonder if she got that off Goody or if Goody got it off her?

Chapter 11

Goody doesn't come in until 9:12. When the lunch bell rings I whip over to her desk.

"Josie was looking for you this morning. She wants to meet you in the park at five today."

She gives me a long, cold stare and then, without a word, gets up. I follow her to the cafeteria, waiting for her to say something. I can see her mental wheels turning all through lunch. I'm anxious to hear the plan, but I don't dare ask about it before she's ready. She barely talks at all and spends most of the meal staring at the picture of the school's malformed panther mascot on the far wall. The only time she looks at me is when I tell her Mom asked me about her Arizona fund.

"It doesn't have a zero balance anymore," Goody says.

"You got money? Pay up! Let's see, you owe me..." I reach for my wallet.

"The money's mine and I'm keeping it. I earned it, believe me."

"By doing chores?" I ask, surprised.

"Nope. I get this money just for taking up space in the world." I look at her quizzically and she grins at me.

"I thought you said you earned it."

"I did. The trick is knowing exactly where to take up space," she says dreamily.

"I don't get it."

"You don't have to," she says, sticking some more fries in her face. "As soon as I get enough of it together, I'm heading south."

I want to ask her more, but something tells me I should just...move on to the next subject.

After school, Goody goes straight home to do her chores. I'm supposed to pick her up at her place at four-thirty so we can go to the park to meet Josie. She still hasn't said if she has a plan. It's not like Goody to be without a plan.

I'm finishing a bowl of cereal when Mom walks in. She's carrying a couple of plastic trays, which she lays on the sofa.

"Help me," she says. I follow her out to the car without my coat on. She hands me a jug. I take it.

"The man at the store kept putting things on the counter and I kept letting him. It's just a notion, you know. That room shouldn't go to waste." I look down at the jug in my hand. Developing fluid. My other hand is holding one of those big timing clocks.

"You're going to make a darkroom out of Dad's office?"

"Don't look so surprised, Stevie. You think it was my big dream to work the Wolfe Island ferry? I used to take lots of snapshots. Your dad bought me a good camera when we were first married. Then we went on vacation, took it to the beach and it got lost. I've used cheap ones since then. I was always going to get another real one... It was fifteen years ago I had that camera. Fifteen years, Stevie. It goes like that."

She snaps her fingers, drops the rest of the stuff on the sofa, takes off her coat and heads for the basement. I stare at the sofa, then down the hall, then at the clock.

I grab my coat and put it on. Mom comes upstairs.

"Where are you going?"

"To the park."

"What's at the park?" She's got one hand on my shoulder and her head is cocked to one side. A small beam of light cuts through the hallway and sparkles off her left eye, which is on me. I look out the window in the front door. It's snowing hard now.

The phone rings. Mom holds up one finger as she goes to get it.

"Lori! You'll never guess what I'm doing." She settles into the couch, pulls the darkroom clock from behind her back and starts twirling its hands around.

I close the front door quietly behind me. The snow is thick. It gathers in the folds of my ski jacket. I look up and let the flakes fall toward my face.

I pull my hood up, tie it tight around my face, hug my arms around me and head up the hill to Goody's place.

Mrs. Pryne opens the front door. She's got a portable phone in her hand. She stands in the doorway and yells, "Goody. It's for you." Then she turns down the hall, leaving the door open. I walk in and close it behind me. I stand on the mat in the front hall and wait. Above me the ceiling creaks under Goody's weight. The air smells like pine.

"You said you'd do it." Mrs. Pryne's voice rises.

Goody appears at the top of the stairs. I can tell she can hear her mom. We stare at each other and listen.

"I don't care what plans you made. You can't treat her like this."

Goody stomps down the stairs.

"This isn't about me," Mrs. Pryne says.

"I'm going, Mom," Goody hollers as she gets her plaid windbreaker from the closet.

"Just a second," Mrs. Pryne says and comes to the kitchen doorway with the phone clutched to her chest. "Don't be gone too long."

Goody turns around and sits on the bottom step to put on her boots. When she's done she looks up at me.

"What are you staring at?" she says.

"Nothing." She pulls her toque over her ears and starts stuffing her hair up into it. It makes her face look smaller. She stands up.

"Bye," she yells and doesn't wait for a response before stepping outside into the flying snow. The wind is up and gives us an excuse not to talk. I chug after her. The snow blows in whirlwinds around my feet. The hill up Patrick Street is steep and hard. I puff up it behind Goody.

Tsula's black rubber boots come into view as we reach the crest. She's on the lookout. She looks over her shoulder toward the playground area. Josie is standing on the top of the slide platform.

We hit the corner and Goody walks right past Tsula like she isn't even there. Tsula falls in beside me. I try to ignore her, but I can feel the cold air heating up between us. I mentally hitch myself to the middle of Goody's back and let her heave me up. She does it easy, too, like she's one of those horses you hitch a wagon to. A Clydesdale. Goody's a Clydesdale. A power horse. She's a power horse all reined-in tight to herself and I'm hitched to her back.

I look at Tsula. Gold eyes or no gold eyes, there's nothing Tsula could say that would shake what I got for Goody and her all-inness, her whip-sharpness, her crush-readiness. I'm hitched to that. I need it. I heed it. It pulls me up.

"What is she wearing on her head?" Josie asks Tsula, loud enough for us all to hear. "Good-for-nothing Pryne presents the latest in ugly, fat-ass girl headgear. You've been reading some strange magazines, girl."

Goody's mouth tightens and curls down at each end, like she's holding back a belch, or smothering a laugh. Josie's arms are braced against the frame at the top of the slide. She's smiling her white Skeletar grin. The spaces between her teeth are dark and wide and the fog of her breath blows out of them.

Josie's eyes flicker the same way Mom's do when she's about to tear up a picture of Dad.

"I heard you want to fight me," Josie says.

"I'm tired of fighting you. I want this thing between you and me settled. How do you want to do that?"

Josie raises her pencil-thin eyebrows and leans forward on the upper rail of the slide platform. Tsula comes up behind her and looks down at me, surprised. I give her the thumbs up. This could actually work.

Then Josie straightens up and pulls on her mitts.

"Why should I want this to be over when it's so obviously getting to you? You're tired of it? Too bad. I'm happy you're suffering. It gives me pleasure to see you in pain." Josie glares down at her enemy.

Goody rubs her hands together. Her torn plaid windbreaker fills to bursting as she breathes in.

She might blow.

Goody steps up onto the end of the orange plastic slide and stomps the snow off her feet. The hollow sound of the slide against Goody's boots keeps all eyes on her as winter rains down around us.

"I'm not in pain, jerkess. I'm over it. It's time to grow up and move on. You decide how to make this be over and I'll agree to it, whatever you come up with. You can't ask for better terms than that. It's on you now."

Goody looks taller and softer at the same time. A lock of hair has worked its way out of her toque and is suspended in the wind beside her face.

Goody makes the peace sign. I swallow hard.

Josie pounds the slide with her heel, then shoots down it at top speed, slamming into Goody with full force. Goody flies a few feet and falls flat on her ass on the frozen sand.

Josie sits at the end of the slide, clutching her sides, laughing. Tsula looks at me. I suck in ice air, go over to Goody and stick my hand out to help her up.

She pushes me off. Her face. Her mental eyes. I instinctively step between her and Josie, take one more look at Goody's calm and protect my head with my arms. She wipes me aside with one easy swipe of her paw and lunges at Josie, punching her in the ear. Josie's head snaps to the side.

A gust of wind blows snow across the playground.

Josie's head wobbles on top of her neck. I swear, I can hear the ringing in her ears as she raises her hand to the side of her face. A ghost of breath leaks out of her open mouth.

Tsula comes out of nowhere and grabs Goody from behind, somehow managing to pin her arms behind her back. Josie's lip is bleeding. She dabs it with her orange mitten, takes a staggered step forward and narrows her watery eyes at Goody.

"Your parents must be so proud," she says. I feel a chill at the back of my neck. Josie licks the blood off her lip, staring at Goody. Waiting.

Goody clears her throat.

"Now your dad can brag to his Kingston Pen cell mates about how his precious daughter is exactly like him. He can tell them how you took me down, just like he took down your uncle. With a lawn chair. *Slam*. Across the head." Goody's spit makes spots on her windbreaker. "You want to kill me, don't you? *Come on.*"

Josie's eyes gleam like white neon. Her lower lip quivers. She's paralyzed except for that lower lip.

Then, it stops. My heart stops. Even the snow seems to stop.

Josie whips off her mitts and flashes forward.

She slaps at Goody's face. Hard. I suck in with each clap of skin on skin. Each hit makes Goody's face open wider with weird happiness. Finally Tsula lets go of Goody to try to stop Josie. The action in front of me seems slow and fast at the same time. Jittery, like an old movie. Even with Tsula between them, Goody manages to sock Josie in the face again. Josie stumbles backwards and falls. Tsula turns to keep Goody away but Goody elbows her in the stomach. Tsula doubles over and has to lean against the tree.

Goody's eyes are all screwy and her jaw is clenched.

She takes another run at Josie, who's still on the ground writhing in pain. Goody raises her tree-trunk leg as if she's going to kick her in the head.

She's going to kill her.

I dive in front of Josie, landing on one knee.

"Goody," I say, holding up my arms to stop her foot from making contact. Tsula screams and Goody's foot stops in mid-air. We lock eyes.

"Hear that, Man Child? Your girlfriend's scared.

Maybe you should go protect her instead, huh?" I can feel Josie still crouched behind me. I look over at Tsula who shakes her head. She heard what Goody said.

"Stop," I say to Goody.

I hear the whip of air before her kick lands hard on my hip. I go down. I stare at the sky. Snowflakes fall on me through the dark sky and it's like I'm flying through space at warp drive and, at the same time, tunneling backwards into the cold ground.

Goody stands over me with blank eyes. I instinctively pull my legs into my chest and cover my head with my arms.

When I'm brave enough to look again, she's gone.

I roll over and feel snow stick to the side of my head. Then I'm barfing by the tree.

I stumble over to the others. At least my leg's not broken.

"You okay?" I ask them. Tsula wraps her arms around Josie. My hip is aching where Goody kicked me.

"That psycho split my lip," Josie moans.

"You're hurt. Maybe I should get my mom," I say. Tsula nods.

"No, pipsqueak. The last thing I need is for my mom to know I've been in a fight. You want her to have a heart attack?"

I rub my side. Josie watches.

"Don't you dare tell anyone about this or I swear to God..." She points at me and makes me look into her hard, angry eyes. "She didn't get me that bad. My mother's got enough problems without hearing about this from your mother."

I sit on the stairs to the slide platform. Tsula whispers something to Josie. Josie shakes her head and puts snow on her lip. We sit there a long time like that, being quiet, getting snowed on. I think about Mom at home talking to Aunt Lorraine about the darkroom. I should have something like that. I should want to do something cool like that.

Eventually, Josie stands up, wipes the snow and dirt off her knees and examines the blood on her mitts. Then she and Tsula start walking. Josie dabs at her lip.

Tsula looks back at me with worried gold eyes. I wave for her to go on. It's not like she's really my girl-friend. I'm never going to forgive Goody for that.

Kicking me was bad enough. Why did she have to call Tsula my girlfriend right in front of her?

After they've gone, I climb under the slide platform and retrieve my blue swatch. It's frozen stiff. I touch it to my cheek. But it doesn't make me feel any better, so I put it back.

When I get home I hear Mom moving in Dad's office. I stand at the top of the basement stairs and pick at the end of the railing with my nails.

"Mom?" I call down.

The moving stops and I hear her blow her nose. I go down a few steps and sit on a stair and lean on the railing because my hip is killing me.

I can see her through the beaded curtain. She's standing in the middle of a bunch of boxes with a dust rag in her hand. She's wiping her nose with her crying apron.

"I've got to make use of what's left, Stevie. It's not to take anything away from you."

"I didn't think that." I climb down the rest of the way, pull the beads aside and look down at the box of magazines.

"We can put them in your room if you want. We could get you some more bookcases."

I shake my head.

"I don't want them," I say and sit down in the chair. My side brushes against the side of the desk and I feel myself wince. Mom's gone back to pulling things out of the filing cabinet and doesn't notice.

"I'm going to leave the records in here," she says. "Like the house insurance and your education fund, but some of this stuff I don't see any reason to keep."

I look at the pile on the desk, the brochures, all Dad's folded-up secret wishes.

"I hate the idea of him sitting down here not doing what he wanted to do. You know what I mean, don't you, Stevie?"

"Yeah."

"I wish he would've got more out of the time he had."

"That's a good wish, Mom." She stares at me like she hasn't in years. I look at the pile of stuff on the table.

I don't want it. That's not him. Wishes aren't real. Wishes are like prayers for stuff that you know can't really happen.

Like I wish Dad were here. Like I wish I didn't go to the park today.

I turn on the desk lamp in my room. It lights up the picture of my dad that sits in the corner by some rocks we picked up on a camping trip to Frontenac Park. In the picture, we're pretend sword-fighting with our hot-dog sticks by the campfire. Fighting and grinning like idiots.

I wonder if Josie's dad is in jail with the drunk driver who ran down Dad. That guy had a daughter, too. I used to be jealous of that guy's daughter.

My wrist is wet from rubbing my eyes. I push the picture of me and Dad back out of the light. I wipe my

nose on my sleeve and close my eyes tight, trying to see the future through the inside of my eyelids.

And something comes to me.

If I ever wanted to stop being friends with Goody, this would be the time.

Chapter 12

The next morning at breakfast I'm eating my oatmeal and thinking about Tsula's gold eyes and how she looked at me last night before she took Josie out of the park.

"How can you tell if someone likes you?" I ask Mom.

She smiles, moves to the sink and turns on the tap. She rinses a pot and then looks back at me over her shoulder. She searches my face with her eyes and looks down at my clothes.

"What?" I say.

"You need new pants. We'll go shopping this weekend."

"So you think my pants make me unlovable?"

"This is about the girl from the library, right?" she asks. I wait and then shrug. "You need new pants."

After breakfast, I check myself out in the bathroom mirror. The bruise on my hip is smudgy blue, like a shadow, and it runs into the bruise on my stomach. I'll be sore for a while.

I avoid the park on my way to school. When I get there, I check for Tsula and Josie, but there's no sign of them. I make my way to the front doors. I'm almost there when Max Revy attacks me from behind.

"Good morning, Man Child," he says. His maple syrup breath covers me as he crowds me into the wall of the school. "You're looking sexy today. Let's feel those muscles." A thick curl of greasy hair sits on his right eye. I notice a rip in the underarm of his coat as he moves in to torture me. He grabs my arm and pinches it. I stand stiff and try not to struggle. I stick my arm out as far as I can to protect my bruised side.

I see Josie and Tsula move along the fence at the other end of the yard. They're walking slowly, deep into whatever they're talking about. Josie shakes her head violently and then stands against the fence with her arms crossed. It looks like Tsula is trying to talk her into something.

Max lets go of my arm. I shift my books from hand to hand and hold the other arm out for him, still watching Josie and Tsula. Josie pushes off the fence, straightens up and moves past Tsula. Tsula calls after her and runs to catch up. Then I notice how quiet it is and look down at my arm. It's still hanging in mid-air, waiting for Max to squeeze it. He's staring at it, too, with his face all screwed up.

"Better do this one, too, Max. Otherwise I'll be off balance." He swipes his hand at it, pushing it out of his face.

"You're already off-balance," he says and walks away. I lean my head against the wall and watch him go.

Josie comes around the corner by herself and grins a skull grin. Her lip is fat and she's got her hair pulled into a short braid that she's drawn over the side of her face that Goody punched.

She's coming right at me, like I'm the one she's looking for.

She stops in front of me, takes me in from top to bottom and then puts her finger to her lips and says, "Shhhhh."

I don't say anything. She moves on as the bell rings. I step into the middle of the yard, rub my arm and feel the wave of students part around me as they march toward the school.

I wait until the last second before going into home room. I keep my head up and make for my seat.

She's there. Goody's seat is right beside mine. I'm careful not to look at her. After the morning announcements, she knocks on her desk to try to get my attention, but I ignore her. Later, when we're sup-

posed to be working on our maps, she throws a pencil crayon at me. I pick it up and use it to color in the Indian Ocean.

"Are you all right?" she asks, like she really wants to know. I feel a hard ball of licorice form at the back of my throat. I turn my chair so my back is toward her.

"You can be mad at me if you like, Stevie. I'm sorry."

I scrape my chair back and the room goes quiet. I move to an empty desk at the back of the room. The rest of the class starts whispering.

Goody's still looking at me. I swallow, bring my head closer to my map and concentrate on making my isotherms beautiful. Goody stands up and the room goes dead silent. Dead. Silent.

"Sit down, Goody. Let it wait until after class," Mr. Pedlar says. She sits down and the room stays hushed for a long, long time, until someone drops an eraser and then the whole class giggles, except me and Goody.

When the bell goes, I whip out of my desk and make for the door.

I'm halfway down the hall when I hear her yell behind me.

"Stevie?"

I don't stop.

This is going to be a very long day.

In French, I catch Max Revy looking back at me. He's got a serious expression on his face, for once, like he's just figured out that I'm human. I motion with my finger for him to turn around in his seat and he does. He sneaks a couple of over-the-shoulder looks at me later. I show him my middle finger and he takes it in, but keeps staring.

"The board is this way, Max," Mrs. Dorosh says, in English. She hardly ever does that.

After the lunch bell, I head for my locker. Tsula's leaning against it.

"You want to eat with us?" she asks.

Just like that, presto, change-o. "So I'm on your team now?" I say to her.

"Why not?" she says. She pulls some lip balm out of her pocket and puts it on. I close my locker. At the end of the hall, I see Goody dialing her combination. Her black sweater is all bunched up at the back of her neck. I can tell she's catching the action in her peripheral vision.

"I thought you hated me," I say to Tsula, and smile for Goody's benefit.

"Not so much." Her quiet voice is like honey. My face goes warm, but I shake my head.

"I can't be part of Josie's let's-get-Goody show. She

shouldn't have…done what she did last night, but you have to admit she was provoked."

"So you're still on her side, then?" Tsula takes a step back and puts her hand on her hips. I look behind me. Josie's at the other end of the hall. I look at Goody. She's staring at me now, waiting.

"Yeah, whose side are you on, Stevie?" she shouts down.

"Mine," I say, loud enough for them all to hear. I thread my lock through the locker, snap it shut and make my way to the cafeteria.

Lunch takes ten years. The guys beside me talk about nothing but hockey. I know that this guy Serge and his buddies can feel me listening, and they don't like it. After ten minutes, Goody gets up from our old table and leaves. I breathe a sigh of relief.

"Bet you're happy to get that weight off your chest," someone whispers in my ear. I turn around and it's Kent. He's sitting across from Bea Fong who, I swear, waves at me from across the table. Kent slaps me on the back. It thunders through me and shakes loose the lump of licorice in my throat so that I almost gag.

I bang my hand against my chest. Kent and the hockey guys think I'm being funny. They're all laughing and it's like I'm in an alternate universe where I'm magically the most popular guy.

Bea Fong waved at me.

I do feel good, like a neutron star's been lifted off my shoulders. I sit up straight and take a long deep breath.

By the end of the day I have seven thousand new friends. Girls are treating me nice. I knew that hanging with Goody was holding me back, but I had no idea that...

I ask this girl, Rosa, if I can borrow one of her pencils and she gives me this sparkly silver one and says I can keep it. Serge punches my arm in the hall and says, "Hey, man," on my way to math. Then I get a question right on the board and this other guy, Martin, gives me the thumbs up on my way back to my seat.

Of course, Goody is there, but I just don't look at her. I make sure I sit someplace where I won't be able to see her.

I can't believe how changed everything is in one single day. Everyone knows I fell out with Goody. Everyone. And they're all on my side.

I'm still dreading the end of the day because me and Goody walk home along the same streets. When the bell goes, I decide to spend a real long time at my locker so that she can get a head start on me. I can see her waiting at the hall corner. She knows I see her, too.

Finally, I can't take it anymore.

"What are you waiting for?" I say to her. The other kids in the hall stop and watch us.

"I thought we were friends, Stevie," she says.

That's the thing with Goody. She puts herself out there. She locks me with her eyes and I'm getting drawn in by her tractor beam, but at the same time I can feel the kids in the hall waiting for me to say something.

"Not anymore," I tell her. I watch as light drains out of her eyes. I leave out the front doors.

No need to look back. I know she's not following me.

☆ ☆ ☆ ☆ ☆ ☆ ☆

Mom's going to get taught how to develop film at this place downtown where you can rent darkroom space. She tells me about it at dinner. She's so excited, I don't want to ruin her good mood by telling her about how me and Goody aren't friends anymore.

"I can't wait. I got some black-and-white film and I'm taking my camera to work tomorrow to snap some shots off the ferry. How come you never sign up for the extra-curricular things, Stevie? There must be lots at the school there."

I've been stuffing my face with ham and she catches me with my mouth full. I point to my bulging cheek and she sighs. She's not wearing her crying apron. I look at the hook on the door to the basement where it usually hangs. It's gone.

"I'm making lots of new friends," I say to her. It's true. She smiles. I haven't seen her this happy since... ever.

I shovel in another mouthful of ham and wait for black licorice to leak out of it, but it doesn't happen. I keep shoveling, but the licorice doesn't hit. I go for a second helping. Then a third. I miss the taste of licorice in my mouth the same way I miss the apron on the door. Like you miss hiccups.

After I finish the dishes, I open the basement door and go down to Dad's office. I didn't think about him all day today. I was too busy thinking about how totally amazing it is that everyone likes me. I still can't believe it. All this time I could have been normal and happy with friends and everything instead of hanging with Goody and feeding licorice to my inner black hole. I hope it's all right with Dad if I think about something new. It feels wrong, in a right way. Like Mom giving up the apron.

Careful of my sore side, I ease myself onto his desk. Developing bins and chemicals line the shelves. The numbers and hands of the darkroom timer glow in the dark and seem to float in the air. The old smell of wet paper is gone. The dust is gone. A new portable phone sits on an old milk crate. The box of magazines sits in the corner by the other side of the door.

It's amazing how a whole person can fit in a box like that. That's what I thought at Dad's funeral.

A huge long tiredness works its way through my body and turns me all to lead. I am liquid lead now.

All this time I've been walking around with that feeling you have the second after you drop the egg, or touch the hot pot with bare hands, or slip on ice. For that one second you feel like you can undo it, like whatever bad thing that happened could unhappen. For two years I've been holding my breath, balancing eggs on trays of black ice.

I take a few deep liquid-lead breaths, and they turn into laughing.

My liquidness has climbed into my eyes and I'm too tired not to be liquid lead here, laughing at myself in the dark room. So I stare at the shady box of magazines in the corner and lie on the desk, biting my hand to try to hold back the laughter.

A crack of light splits the room as the basement door creaks open.

"Are you all right?" Mom asks. I can't hold it back anymore. I'm shaking and snorting, holding my poor bruised side in stitches. She comes down and turns on the light. It's so bright that I cover my eyes at first, but when I take my hand away, the look on her face peeking through the beaded curtain sets me off again.

"What's so funny?" she says, coming into the room, but I can't answer her. She sits down at the desk, puts her hand on my knee and brushes my hair out of my eyes. "Tell me the truth, Stevie. Are you on drugs?"

Then that's it. I'm hysterical. And the more worried she looks, the worse I laugh.

Chapter 13

Morning. The air's crisp and clean. The sky is blue in that way you see it in those old westerns. The sky is a completely fake blue sky and it makes the branches of the big trees in Skeleton Park look like they've been cut out of black construction paper, like they're popping out of the fake blue sky. I drink in the fall air and feel it work its way down to my toes.

I'm growing. I can feel it.

I smile at a lady walking her dog and she smiles back. I go up Ordnance Street instead of walking through the park. It still borders on the park, but it's as far out of my way as I'm willing to go.

When I get up by the park I look across it.

Goody's there on the swings. I hike up my knapsack and walk on by. She follows me with her eyes and gets up as I reach the corner.

"Stevie," she calls.

I stop. Might as well get this over with. I let her catch up to me and then start walking at a fast pace.

"Am I done being punished yet?" she asks, pretending like I wasn't perfectly clear yesterday. I stop and cross my arms. She puts her hands on her hips, like I'm the one who did something wrong. "I asked you a question," she says.

"You aren't being punished. I told you, Goody, we aren't friends anymore." Her eyes go hard.

"Why? So you can fart around with those plebeians?"

"You know why."

"Okay. I wanted a chance to explain about that." Her hands fall from her hips and she takes a deep breath. She has a leaf on the elbow of her black sweater. I'm tempted to brush it off, but keep my arms crossed.

"I'm so sorry about that, Stevie. I don't know what happened. I think there's a small chance that I might be just the tiniest bit insane, and I've got a date with the school counselor to talk about it. I'm going to confess everything, and if they want to hand me over to the police, that's fine. I know it was wrong what I did. Even to Josie, even though she pushed me first. But... you know, Stevie. You know I just wanted to make it all be over."

The wind is up and blows her frizzy hair around the edges of her toque. I press my lips together and shake my head.

"I can't," I say.

"You can't what?" she demands.

"I can't be friends with you anymore," I say, and my eyes well up all sudden so I have to lift my head back.

"You're too much, Goody." My voice cracks. "You're just way, way too much." I wipe my eyes on my sleeve. "Please, just leave me alone, all right?"

Her face. I can't stand it. I start walking and then stop again. "And don't bother confessing. Josie doesn't want the police involved. She thinks it'll freak her mom out. You wanted it over, so let it be over, all right?"

I wait for her to nod and when she finally does, I turn my back on her for good.

Then I run. I run on the road through the cool wind and the red leaves falling through the fake blue sky.

In French, Max Revy sits behind Goody and knocks the back of her chair with his Nikes. She lets him. It's incredible how that guy knows who's ripe to be picked on.

Then, in the middle of this other kid conjugating a verb, Goody stands up and kicks her chair into the aisle. Mrs. Dorosh asks her to sit down. Goody shakes her head and aims her thumb back at Max.

"Max," Mrs. Dorosh says and makes Max sit beside her at the front. A couple of kids look at me. I keep my eyes on my binder.

At lunch I sit beside the hockey guys again. Goody sits by herself with her two orders of fries and gravy. Serge asks me what my dad does so I have to explain about him being dead. The hockey guys all look down at their food.

"That's rough," Serge says, and then all the guys chime in saying how rough it must be for me. The thing is, Serge already knew about my dad. It was in the papers and the teachers made a point of talking about drunk driving in class. I know why he asked me about it, though. It's because that's how they need to see me, as the kid whose dad got done in by a drunk driver. Now that I'm not friends with Goody, they have to re-label me, and this is the sign they're hanging around my neck: Father, dead.

I sneak a look over at Goody. It doesn't seem to bother her, sitting alone.

On my way to English, I spot Goody sitting on the bench outside the counselor's office. I walk over just as the bell rings.

"Don't worry," she says. "I won't say anything about what happened at the park. I couldn't just

cancel my appointment. They'd be suspicious. I'll talk about something else."

"Like what?"

"Gee, I can't think what other problems I might have," she says, cocking her head sideways and twisting her finger hard into her cheek. I take off for English and spend the whole class worrying about what Goody's saying in there.

Goody's mom is waiting for her in the car after school. Goody's standing at the bottom of the stairs. Enough kids are pouring out the front doors that Mrs. Pryne hasn't spotted her yet. Or maybe she has, but she's not doing anything about it and Goody doesn't seem in any hurry to get to the car, even though it's drizzling out. She just stands there staring as the car belches exhaust into the wet air. She sighs. Droplets dot the frizzy ends of her hair.

She sees me and starts moving toward the car. Just before she gets there, she turns and gives me the peace sign. I feel my black hole yawn.

Space hangs like haze in the room when I open my eyes in the middle of the night. What was I dreaming? I can't remember but I think Dad was in it. I pull the covers up over my cold shoulders and listen to the quiet of the night. After a minute, I become aware of music playing down the street. Someone is having a party. The clock reads 2:47.

I crawl out of bed and make my way to the window to look at the stars. I stare up, trying to pick them out. I find Polaris, the North Star, the one that all the others seem to move around. I lie on the floor and keep my eyes on it.

That's where Mom finds me in the morning – lying on the floor with my rag rug pulled over me.

"What are you doing down there?"

"I must have fallen out of bed," I tell her. Then I remember. "We going shopping today?"

The salesgirl at the department store is Lisa, Bea Fong's older sister. Mom's saying how we should get me some underwear while we're here and I'm screaming with my eyes for her to stop. She looks over her shoulder at Lisa and then gets it.

I grab a pair of jeans off the shelf and make my way to the fitting rooms. I have to pass Lisa to get there.

"Hey, Stevie," she says.

"Hey." I didn't even know she knew my name.

I try the jeans on and I'm drowning in them. I look in the mirror. I look like an elf. A featherweight in heavyweight's clothing. I punch at the mirror.

"How's it going?" asks Lisa, knocking on the change room door.

"Come out, Stevie. Let me see," Mom calls, and I see the knob jiggle.

"Step away from the door," I snap.

"Do you need a smaller size?" Lisa asks. I move to the corner of the teeny room and try to squeeze my head into it.

"Stevie?" Mom calls.

I gather myself and jump around into a karate stance.

"Leave me now," I tell the door. "I will solve the pants problem on my own. Thank you for your cooperation. That is all." I hear a shuffle in front of the door and some whispering. Then they leave. I put on my old pants and come out. Mom and Lisa are talking at the counter. I scoot to the shelves, help myself to several pairs of jeans in assorted styles and colors and quickly pick out nine shirts and three sweaters. I tip-toe back to the dressing room, lock the door and go to work.

This time I've chosen better. I look good. Especially in the sweaters. With no one standing beside me, I almost look like I could be tall. Dad was almost tall. Maybe I'll be almost tall, too. Maybe I'll be taller than him, even, now that I've started growing.

I pick out two pairs of pants and three tops,

including a turtleneck sweater that makes me look taller. I put on my favorite outfit and go out to show Mom. When I walk out there, Bea Fong and Kent are standing by the counter talking with Mom and Lisa.

"Stevie," Bea says happily. Lisa and Mom turn around. Mom actually claps her hands when she sees me.

"You look real good," she says. Kent's checking me out, assessing my outfit. Mom moves over to stand closer to Bea and Lisa. "Looks like we're getting you outfitted just in time, Stevie. Maybe some girl will think you're cute." Mom nudges Lisa with her elbow.

My throat begins to close up. The girls exchange a look and giggle, like they might have someone in mind for me. Kent raises his eyebrows, sticks out his lower lip and seems to consider the possibility that I, Squeak Stevie Walters, soon to be ex-Man Child, might, perhaps, possibly be thought of as cute by some girl – and then he shakes his head.

I jump into my karate stance and slice the air with my hands. The girls burst out laughing. I fake fight my way back into the fitting room, lock the door and slump against it to catch my breath.

"That was good," I hear Bea tell my mom.

I made Bea Fong laugh. I lean into the mirror and

fog it up with my breath. Then I draw a happy face in the fog.

That *was* good.

We're looking at gloves when I spot Goody in Men's Wear coats. I step behind a rack of hats so she won't see me. She's with an older man who is wearing a long leather overcoat with a tie belt. He's big like her, but not in the same way. He's tall and broad, with dark slicked-back hair and gold-rimmed sunglasses that are hanging from the corner of his mouth as he checks out a price tag on a red ski jacket.

Mr. Pryne, I presume.

He peels the red ski jacket off the hanger and Goody shakes her head. He unzips it, his sunglasses still hanging from his mouth. He holds it up for her and she sticks her arms in it. The shoulders are huge on her. She looks like a gigantic tomato. Mr. Pryne takes a step back and scratches the arm of his sunglasses into his chin. He makes a zipping motion in the air with his hand. The coat is way too big up top, but it's tight around Goody's hips. She's a tomato wearing a girdle. Mr. Pryne sighs and goes back to shuffling through the rack. He has one of those stubbly beards that used to be popular five years ago.

"I have to go to the washroom," I tell Mom.

"When did mitts come to cost so much?" she answers, looking at a price tag.

"The prices have gone up since the last millennium, Mom."

"What?" she says.

"That's the last time we went shopping." She slaps me on the arm with a pair of Isotoners.

"Go pee. I'll meet you in Housewares. I need to find something for your aunt for Christmas."

I make my way through the racks, keeping my eye on Goody. I creep around the wall by the cash register in Men's Wear and pretend to be looking at some corduroy jackets.

The saleswoman walks up to Mr. Pryne. Goody's taken off the red ski jacket. She draws her hands into the sleeves of her old windbreaker and lets her hair fall in front of her face.

"Can I help you find anything?" the saleswoman asks Mr. Pryne.

"Yes," he says. "We're looking for a coat for my daughter."

"Women's coats are up the escalator to your right," she says. Mr. Pryne puts his hand on a rack and leans into it.

"See?" Goody mumbles. Her father closes his eyes and shakes his head.

"No. We've been up there and now we're looking

here," he says to her, pointing at the ground. Then he inhales deeply and addresses the saleswoman. "You see, I'm divorced, so I'm new at this. She said she wanted a ski jacket, something a little sporty. But because she's a big girl, they don't have anything like that in her size upstairs, so I thought we'd come down here." When he talks about Goody's size, he widens the space between his hands, letting his sunglasses dangle between his fingers. Goody stands beside him, looking at her shoes and holding her arms tight against the sides of her windbreaker to hide the rips at her hips.

"As you can see, though, we aren't having any luck," Mr. Pryne says. "But if she goes home without a new coat, her mother will take me to court." He throws his arms up in the air and laughs this huge fake laugh.

He's so loud, people turn to look at him. Goody stands perfectly still, with a stone-cold face and hurt eyes.

My hand tightens around the leather button of an M-sized tan corduroy jacket.

The saleswoman, who is an older woman with loose gray hair, looks sympathetically at Goody and then holds up her finger.

"I think we may have just the thing in the back," she says. She walks toward me and I lower my head. I can see the woman's lips tighten as she reaches for the phone. Mr. Pryne takes out his cell phone and checks for messages. Goody turns her back on him and pets the fake fur collar on a big blue jacket. Her hair hangs over her face. I see her reach under the fringe of it with the back of her hand and wipe her cheek.

I hear the saleswoman on the phone. "Can you bring down a couple of size 22 jackets, plain colors, black or blue? I've got an asshole down here. I'll meet you at the elevator so it looks like I went to the back. Doesn't matter. If it fits she'll take it." The woman hangs up the phone, looks at me and plasters on a smile. "Are you finding everything you need?"

I nod.

She walks back toward Goody and her father and that's when Goody spots me. Our eyes meet and I can see the corners of her mouth tremble. I can't take it. I speed around the back of the cash table and nearly bang into the saleswoman on her way to the elevator.

"Sorry," I say to her. I have to go around Goody and Mr. Pryne to get to Housewares. I wander back into belts and ties to put as much distance between us as possible. I knock against some belts and their buckles clack together. Goody looks over at me. She must see the pity on my face because she stiffens right up and gives me the finger.

Just as I pass them I hear Mr. Pryne say, "Don't

they have any sports teams at school you can join? Basketball's good exercise. I bet that'd be fun for you. You could make some new friends to go shopping with. I'd give you money for it. Where did that woman go?" He looks at his watch, rests his arms on top of a rack and puts on his sunglasses.

I hustle on, keeping my eye on the finger behind Goody's stiff back.

I take the escalator one floor up and sit on a display bed in the sheet section. I feel like I did the first time Goody hit me, like all my breath's been sucked out of me and into another universe.

I lay my head on the huge stack of display pillows and stare up at the fluorescent lights. After fifteen minutes I get up and go looking for Mom. I find her in the lingerie section.

And I give her a big hug for not being the slightest bit like the Prynes.

Chapter 14

I'm halfway through making carrot and raisin muffins when I realize I don't have enough oil. I get some cash off Mom and make my way up to The Store Famous. It's stopped raining and now there's a sheer layer of ice over the sidewalks and the road. I nearly fall on my butt just stepping off the front stoop.

I almost decide to turn back, but I really want to make the muffins. Now that the licorice taste is gone, I want to bulk up, and baked goods seem to be the way to go. I'm going to be big and buff and maybe even take up karate. I seem to have good balance for that.

My balance is tested all the way up Patrick Street. The hill is especially challenging, and I have to walk on people's lawns where the grass cracks and melts under my feet. When I get up to the corner of the park, I stand up straight and stretch my back out.

"Scratching your ass, Squeak?" Josie calls over

from where she's sitting on top of the picnic table. Tsula's beside her holding a big red and yellow beach umbrella. The rest of the park is empty. Tsula's dark choppy hair is pulled back behind one ear with a pink metallic barrette. She smiles as I get closer.

"Hello, enemies," I call.

"That's funny," says Josie sarcastically. She adjusts her feet on the seat of the picnic table. The glow of the umbrella makes them look like they're in sunlight.

"What are you guys doing here?"

"My brother's girlfriend is visiting and they are being so disgusting we had to get out of my place, but Josie forgot her key so we're locked out until her uncle gets back from Food Basics," Tsula says. Josie socks her on the side.

"You don't have to tell him everything," she says. I wonder if that's the same uncle that Josie's father beat up. He must have been hurt bad if it got Josie's dad sent to the Penitentiary.

Tsula switches hands with the umbrella, realizes it's not raining, takes it down and starts poking at the holes in the picnic table with it. She's checking me out. I'm wearing my new turtleneck sweater. I rack my brain for something to say.

"Goody said she wouldn't tell about the fight," I tell them.

Josie looks at me suspiciously and then sits up a

bit. Tsula's still checking me out. I tuck my chin into the turtleneck of the sweater the way I practiced in the change room.

"Tsula, go see if the car's in the driveway yet. I want to talk to Stevie," Josie says. Tsula goes to get up.

"Wait," I say. "Why can't she hear what you have to say?"

"It's private," Josie says.

"You trust me more than you trust her? Anything you say, I'll tell her later anyway, just on principle," I spit out. "Why are you keeping secrets from your best friend anyway? Did you know about her dad, Tsula?" I can feel licorice trying to work its way into my throat but I squash it down. I'm not going to be that way anymore. I'm not going to be scared. I'm going to say what I think.

I can tell Josie feels it off me, too. She crosses her arms. Tsula looks at her sideways and then at me.

"I thought her dad was working computers in the Nigerian consulate," says Tsula. Josie looks away, into the park.

"You were afraid Tsula would tell about your dad? Or were you waiting for Goody to spill it for you? She kept your secret for two years, Josie. She protected you even though you were at her every single day."

"Stop it." Josie stands up on the seat of the picnic table. It's raining again. She's looking around the park deciding whether to take off and wiping her face with wet hands. We wait while she dries her face on the inside of her coat collar.

Tsula opens the umbrella and holds it up high enough to shelter all three of us. I step in under it so she can lower her arm. I can hear the drops falling all around us. Our breaths hang heavy in the afternoon mist.

"For your information Goody wasn't protecting me. She was protecting herself over what she did," Josie says.

"What did she do?" I ask. Josie laughs weakly.

"She called the cops on my dad," she says, narrowing her eyes. "It's her fault he's in jail."

I look at Tsula. She didn't know either.

"But he beat up your uncle," I say.

"You weren't there. You don't know what happened. She had no business sticking her nose in it. You never have arguments at your house? Your dad never yell?" Josie snaps.

"No. He never did," I say. I see her remember that my dad is dead.

"We could have handled it. My mom could have calmed him down. He didn't hit my uncle that bad. He wouldn't have even gone to jail if he wasn't on probation for stuff he did a million years ago. My uncle was so drunk he doesn't even remember what they were fighting about, so it wasn't like a real fight. If

Goody didn't call the cops, my uncle wouldn't have pressed charges. He never did before. It was no big deal. If Goody wasn't there, they would have gone to bed and the next morning it would have been like nothing ever happened." Josie looks from my face to Tsula's and back again, tightly clenching her skull jaw.

"Now you know. Satisfied? You can go home," she says. Then she stands up and walks away without even looking at Tsula.

When we get to my place, I put on the kettle. Mom's downstairs. I can hear the beads on the doorway rattling. I go to the top of the basement stairs and yell down that I'm home.

"Can you help me, Stevie?" she asks. She's standing on a milk crate trying to unscrew the beads from the doorway.

"I got a friend, Mom," I say. "You want some tea?"

"Goody's here?" She puts down her screwdriver and wipes her hand on her butt.

"No, someone else. I'm making tea. Can I bring some down to you?" I say, emphasizing the word down. She catches it. Her eyes widen and she loses her balance a little.

"Is it that girl?" she whispers loudly. I look behind me at Tsula. She heard it.

"Yes, it's Tsula, Mom. Tea?" She picks up her screwdriver again and wags it at me.

"That would be lovely, Stevie," she says in her company voice.

I pull out three of the good green mugs from the cupboard and blow inside them to make sure they aren't dusty. Tsula is sitting in Dad's chair. I'm having a hard time looking at her now that we're out of the rain. She's too clear. I put out the nice milk and sugar set and spread some digestive cookies on a plate. I forgot to get the oil for the muffins.

"This is interesting wallpaper. Snow on log cabins," she says. "It's cozy. Usually wallpaper's all flowers or fancy designs."

I accidentally look at her and she smiles. I move my eyes to the wallpaper and the bright yellow light coming from the windows of the tiny log cabins.

"I used to pretend that I lived there." I prop my butt against the counter, waiting for the kettle.

"What's it like inside?" she asks, and her gold eyes shine like the light in the log cabin window.

I stare at the wallpaper and let myself do what I used to do when Dad sat where Tsula is now, and Mom cooked, and I balanced my feet on the rung of my chair, ate my hot dogs with my fingers and only half listened to them talk.

"When you open the door of the cabin the first

thing you notice is how warm it is. It smells like burning because there's a wood stove over under where that chimney is. Sometimes I put a fireplace instead of a wood stove. You take off your boots, carry them over to the heat, peel off your socks and sit on the rocking chair to dry your toes. Behind you is a long wood table that's in the center of the room. My dad sits at it reading an old paperback. Mom mixes cookie batter and you can hear the wood spoon bang against the side of the big brown bowl."

"It sounds good, Stevie," Tsula says and makes me look at her. I get busy making the tea. I pour out Mom's and take it down to her. She's in the laundry room putting clothes in the dryer. I put her mug on the shelf behind her and dart back upstairs before she can say anything.

I sit across from Tsula and push the plate of digestives toward her. She takes one, bites it and crumbs fall onto her sweater.

"What are we going to do, Stevie?" she asks me.

"Nothing. It's over," I say. She shakes her head. I know she's right. It will never be over between Goody and Josie. At least now I know why. I pour us some tea and we both watch the steam from it curl into the kitchen air. Mom's knocking around downstairs. The noise makes it easier to sit with Tsula.

"If Josie didn't want Goody to tell about her dad

being in jail, how come she was always at her? She was daring Goody to spill it."

Tsula rubs her finger over the letters printed on the digestive cookie. "I think Josie was like, 'Just say it, bitch. Let's get this over with.' Or, you know, like picking at a scab – testing to see if it's healed. Only with Josie always picking at it, the whole thing never got a chance of healing."

Tsula's been like me in this thing. We're both in the background of it, like wallpaper, but we're also always there watching those two tear each other apart. At least, that's the way it was before Goody spilled about Josie's dad. Who knows what will happen now.

"Did Josie's dad beat up his own brother?"

"No. It was her mother's brother. He lives with them now. He helps them. I think having him around is hard on her. She really misses her dad. She said so all the time, only I thought he was in Nigeria."

Tsula looks down at her cookie and smooths its rough edges.

"He must have gone to jail right after I met her. I was new at that school then. Josie kind of picked me to hang out with."

She grins. I swear, the lights in the cabin windows shine off her eyes.

"I knew those two had some sort of fight going on. Josie said that she was sick of Goody being jealous of her all the time and she just didn't want to be friends with her anymore. It did seem a little mean of Josie. But, you know, it's hard to feel bad for Goody because she's so…"

"Goody," I add.

"It was easy to see why Josie didn't want to hang with her. It took me a long time to figure out that something else must have happened with them and by then I was close friends with Josie and I…"

"Was trapped," I say. She nods and reaches for another cookie, nibbling the edges all the way around, then dipping the middle into the mug of tea.

The light in the room changes. I look out the back window. A strip of blue cuts through the dark gray clouds, making a long, straight line in the sky. I can see far away.

I turn toward Tsula and slap the table. "This has to do exactly and personally with us." She raises her dark eyebrows and nods into her mug. "Goody asked me if I knew a way we could end the fighting between her and Josie and I just thought of something."

"Yeah? What?"

"She had the right idea with diplomacy, but she didn't really have anything to bargain with. Josie was never going to believe Goody would keep quiet about her dad forever. Man, I can't believe I didn't think of this sooner." I'm so excited I jump in my chair and spill tea on my new sweater. I run to the sink and grab a cloth. I wipe off my sweater and turn to Tsula, grinning like an idiot. "So you want to try?"

"Try what? I don't know what you're talking about. Diplomacy? What do we have to bargain with?"

"Us! We've got us. If Goody wants to be my friend, she has to apologize to Josie. If Josie wants to be your friend, she has to make it up with Goody."

Tsula puts down her tea and looks out the window. She's thinking about it. I work on cleaning my sweater and wait.

"What if Josie doesn't go for it? You and Goody aren't really friends anymore anyway. I can't do that to Josie. She needs me."

"I bet she wants this to be over as badly as Goody does. Don't you think? They just couldn't figure out how to stop it."

"I don't know. I think they sort of liked it."

"But I don't like it and neither do you," I say. If I could do this for Goody...

My mind goes back to how she looked at lunch the other day. It's like Goody knows she's alone in the universe, and because she knows the rules of the universe she knows she can't expect anyone to do anything for her, so she just sits and eats and doesn't even bother to look at me.

I wanted to be normal, but this is more important.

Tsula's staring into her cup. She has crumbs on her top.

"We have to try, at least," I say.

"What exactly do you want to try?" Tsula says, looking up at me.

"We get them to sit down with us in a public place and talk this out," I start, feeling it out as I go. "No fighting or insults allowed, or we leave the table. They stop trying, we leave the table. As long as they try we sit at the table and we sit there until they figure it out. We'll do it in the cafeteria tomorrow at lunch so if anything goes wrong, the cafeteria lady's there to stop it."

Finally she nods.

We work out the details, taking a break only to help Mom hang the new door on the darkroom. We spend the last few minutes saying how things might be after, but we don't get very far because neither one of us can imagine a world in which Josie and Goody get along. It's like imagining peace in the Middle East. It just doesn't figure.

Chapter 15

Goody's front stoop is icy, and I have to hold onto the pillar to keep from slipping. Mrs. Pryne answers the door. Her hair is down, making her look a lot more like Goody. They both have a way of looking at me like I'm the subject for some science experiment.

I nearly slip again and grab onto the pillar with both arms. The expression on Mrs. Pryne's face doesn't shift one iota.

"Is Goody home?" She considers my question and backs into the hallway.

"Come in, Steven." So she does know who I am. "Wait here. I'll go see if she's receiving visitors." She leaves me in the hall and makes her way upstairs. Usually she just calls up.

Mrs. Pryne comes down the stairs and stands in front of me. "You can go up." Then she takes my coat, hangs it in the hall closet and waits until I take off my boots, which she takes from me and lines up on the mat beside Goody's. I wait to see if there's anything else we need to do. She raises her arm to usher me upstairs. I nod and climb.

When I get to Goody's room, the door is closed. My hands are shaking. I knock.

"Come in," she says. I open the door and she's sitting at her desk with her chair turned to face me.

I scout the room. Posters of deep space, pictures of nebulas ripped from magazines, a big blown-up color copy of the Andromeda Galaxy framed on the desk, solar system mobile, handcrank radio, log book. Nothing's changed.

"So?" she says.

"I saw you shopping yesterday."

"*Why* are you here?" Her black sweater is creeping up her back so she looks hunched.

"Did you get a coat?"

"*Next subject.* I thought we weren't friends anymore." Her voice catches at the end like I've never heard it.

"Do you want to be friends?" I move to her bed, sit in the middle of it and cross my legs. The question hangs in front of Goody like a swinging noose.

"Why?" she asks. Her dry lips click together. Her face pulls open my black hole.

She is too much. She's too Goody. If you shaved her frizzy hair off, you'd find a tattoo of the skull and crossbones. Warning: Contents under pressure.

I shimmy my butt to the edge of the bed and hold out my hand to her. She immediately slaps it away. I shake off the slap and reach my hand out again, trying to catch her eyes.

"It's not a trick," I say. "It's a plan. You in?" My outstretched hand sits still in the air between us. She's staring at it. She can't look me in the eye. Her jaw is slack. She's breathing through her mouth. She's blinking back tears.

I reach my hand out farther. She still can't take it. Her hands are clenched on the vinyl arm rests of her desk chair.

"Don't you trust me, Goody?"

That cracks her. She lets out a sob that echoes against the wall behind me. She snaps a hand over her mouth to keep the rest in and bows her head so I can't see her. Her big body heaves and quakes.

My eyes come hot and itchy.

I squat in front of her and stick the hand right under her nose. She hits it twice, then takes it. I hold fast and turn her hand over in mine. Her nails are short, red around the sides and white from holding on so tight. I get up still holding her hand, stand behind the chair and put my arm around her. She keeps a hand over her mouth to stop her mother from hearing her, so that it takes a long time for her to calm down because it's like she's crying inside out.

When she's done, I go sit on the bed again. Her green eyes glow out of the hot pinks of her whites.

"Get me some Kleenex, dumb ass," she whispers. I hand her the box from her bedside table and she parks it in her lap. After she's cleaned up, she lifts her head.

"I saw Josie and Tsula in the park today. I know you called the cops on Josie's dad," I tell her. Goody's eyes try to pull curtains across themselves. She wipes her nose and stares at the Kleenex in her hand.

"I know she thinks I did it to get back at her but that wasn't it." Goody hesitates. "I had to do it." Her face is burning. She tucks her hair behind her ears and drops her hands to her lap.

"Before it happened. We were upstairs at her place. We were arguing. Josie and me. I never went over to her place, she always came here. I didn't know how things were at her place. If only I didn't go there..." She looks up at me.

"The August before grade seven, I came home from camp and the parents told me they were getting separated. Actually, it was Mom who told me because Dad was already gone. They didn't think I needed to know while I was at camp. They thought they were shielding me.

"It didn't seem real at first. It was like Dad was on a long conference. Only it kept getting longer and longer and longer and he wasn't calling and Mom was holed up in her room and she looked about ready to spit any time I tried to talk to her.

"So who am I going to talk to about this, right? My bestest friend, Josie. She would come over and we sat in the back yard and made fun of my parents and how stupid my dad is and how my mom would get over it eventually. And then, once, we were talking about my parents and Josie goes, 'Can't we talk about anything else?' in this whiney voice. I thought she was bored with me. I swear, I didn't know that her dad had all these problems. I didn't know he was on probation. She was always bragging about him doing stuff for her. Taking her to restaurants. Buying her CDs. All I could see was how good she had it and how she couldn't stand to hear about my problems. Next thing you know she's hooked up with Tsula who was this totally new person that she hardly knew and suddenly Josie's going everywhere with her."

Goody pauses and squeezes her pillow.

"I thought she was shutting me out. I went over to her place that night to confront her where she wouldn't be able to squirm out of it. Her dad answered the door and he did seem nice. He had a beer in his hand, but so what? He called her pumpkin. She was not happy to see me. I told her she was weak. I told her she couldn't know what it was like for me and that the least she could do was have a little sympathy. She said she wasn't going to pretend to feel sorry for me. She called me a broken-home crybaby. And I called her a spoiled little daddy's girl."

Goody stares straight ahead at the galaxies on the wall.

"Then we heard glass smashing outside and loud swearing. We ran to the window and there was Josie's dad swinging a lawn chair around his head. Her uncle was already lying on the patio with a broken beer bottle beside him. You should have seen the look on his face. He was so scared. He put his hand up and *whack*." Goody flings her pillow hard onto the bed. "Josie's dad smacked him with the chair. He tried to crawl away but her dad pulled him back by his legs. Then Josie's dad lifted the lawn chair above his head again and Josie pulled me away from the window. She didn't want me to see. I got her off me, ran down the hall, picked up the portable phone, locked myself in the bathroom and called 911. Josie knew what I was doing. She banged on the door yelling at me to stop. The operator answered fast. I told her what was going on. I heard Josie yelling through the window that I had called the cops. I guess her dad stopped then. I stayed locked in the bathroom. Josie sat on the other side and made me promise I wouldn't tell anyone what had happened. She wanted me to tell the police I made a mistake. I said I wouldn't do that, but I swore that I wouldn't tell anyone else... I stayed in there until I heard a police radio outside." She sniffs loudly and wipes her nose on the sleeve of her sweater, trailing a web of goo down her forearm.

"When I opened the bathroom door, Josie was there with this look on her face. I knew I really wrecked it with her. I didn't talk to anyone for a long time after that. No one notices if you do that, by the way. I went three days without saying a single word and no one noticed. I just did my chores and sat out back on the picnic table looking up at the stars. Thank God."

"For the stars?"

"No, Expletive. Thank God I met you."

The light is leaving the room. I turn on the bed-side lamp. Goody rubs her eyes.

"Okay, give it to me. What did you and Tsula come up with?" She smiles her evil, knowing smile and it makes me feel at home.

She's not as hard to convince as I thought she'd be. It's like the fight's gone out of her.

It's almost too easy.

When I leave, Mrs. Pryne meets me at the door, helps me on with my coat and passes me my boots. I forgot to ask Goody what she told the school counselor. It's obvious that someone has had words with the Pryne parental units.

"Good day," I say to Mrs. Pryne when she opens the door for me. She nods her head. I walk carefully across the icy threshold.

As soon as I clear the front path of the house, I take off for home. The giant maples on Raglan Street rain red leaves on me and it feels like confetti in a hero's parade. The street's empty, so I wave my hand to my adoring fans and jog on to the even greater victory that awaits me.

My coat's still on when I call Tsula. Their voice mail picks up right away. Her brother is probably on the phone with his girlfriend. After the beep, I say, "This is a message for Tsula. It's Stevie. Phase one is complete."

It takes forever for her to get back to me. I don't even go to the bathroom in case she calls while I'm in there. I chew my cheese sandwich in small bites so that I won't be caught with food in my mouth when she calls. The licorice taste is completely gone now.

I pull out my wallet and check out the taped-up pictures of my dad. There's the one Mom ripped when I stole twenty dollars from her purse to go to Lake Ontario Amusement Park, and the one from when I told Uncle Burt to f-off under my breath when he

asked if I was shaving yet. I'm so used to looking at Dad's face with the tear marks across it, when I see untorn pictures of him they kind of look wrong.

I go through the photos, running my thumb across the Scotch-taped edges, letting the sticky stuff glom onto my nail. Then I take the blue swatch of cloth out of its compartment and rub it against my face.

The swatches are from Dad's car. Before the funeral, I told Uncle Burt I wanted to see it. Mom was busy with Aunt Lorraine getting things ready at the house. My uncle called the cops and found out where they took Dad's car and he took me there. I cut the swatches out of the driver's seat. I brought a steak knife with me to do it with.

Uncle Burt didn't say anything. He knew I needed them. What I really wanted was the other half of the piece of licorice, but they threw that out. Maybe if I could've eaten that, that would've worked to make me feel like part of Dad was still with me. But it didn't happen that way.

The ringing jolts me. I drop the swatch and dive for the phone. It's Tsula.

"Josie's not going for it. She said she doesn't see why she has to do anything at all, that the whole plan seems designed only to help Goody. She said you were brainwashing me."

"Goody said she'd do it," I say hopefully.

"She has nothing to lose."

"Neither does Josie."

Tsula's not buying it. I'm frustrated for me and Goody both. I feel bad about what happened, but Josie can't go on blaming everyone else for what her dad did.

"She just wants to keep the fight going because as long as it's going she doesn't have to admit to herself that Goody did the right thing by calling the cops."

Tsula stops chewing her gum.

"I think I need to be on her side, Stevie." I can feel myself losing her again.

"Don't decide anything now. Think about it. Me and Goody will be at the table tomorrow and you can come or not. Okay?" I listen to her breathe. I love the sound of her breath in my ear.

"All right," she says. "I'll see you tomorrow."

Mom comes down the stairs. Her hair is all smushed. She's been napping. She stops on the stairs and looks at me.

"Who was that?"

"Tsula." She gives me this quizzical look. I debate whether or not to tell her about the whole sorry mess while she stares at me. Just when I decide to tell her, she takes another step down and then, somehow, it's too late.

Goody's waiting for me at the swings on Monday morning.

She's wearing a big black janitor's coat, or that's what it looks like. The shoulders are humongous, and when she stands up, the shiny ski jacket material drops flat almost to her knees.

It's a man's coat. A big man's coat. It's still snug in the hips.

"That's what he got you?"

"Shut up. Tell me what Josie said."

"She isn't going for it."

"I knew it. See? Nothing works with her. You thought it was me but it never was. She doesn't want it to be over." Goody gets up and starts marching through the park. I watch the sides of her big-ass coat ripple with every step. I count the seconds it takes her to realize I'm not following her. She makes it all the way to Ordnance Street before she turns around. Her mouth is half open. She was so sure I was right behind her, she was even talking to me.

I wave to her from the swings.

She taps her foot. I start swinging. The chains on the swing are so cold they stick to my hands. My knapsack weighs on my back as I lean toward the ground. I close my eyes and listen to the wind in my ears. I concentrate on pumping, one, two, three.

When I open my eyes, she's in front of me with her

arms at her sides, her big coat making her look all stiff and stunned. I cruise to a stop.

"You agreed to this yesterday not because you wanted it, but because you thought Josie wouldn't go for it. Is that right?" I say.

Goody claps her hands together. Slowly. Three times.

"Very good, Stevie. You've been paying attention."

"Would you still agree to the plan if Josie changed her mind?"

"She's not going to." The wind blows her frizzy hair across her face and she flips it out of her eyes to look down on me.

"Promise me that you'll sincerely agree to go through with this when Josie changes her mind. Promise?" She smirks. I stand firm. "No matter what, it's never going to be how it was before," I tell her, pointing at the slide. "You want to show you're sorry for what happened here, for beating her up and kicking me?" Her face goes dark. "Be sorry then. Really be sorry. You haven't tried that yet. Promise me, Goody."

The air around her goes extra still. She's glaring at me and I'm mesmerized by the sharp steel edges of her green eyes cutting through me.

"I promise," she says softly. Her frizzy hair is caught in one side of the big coat's collar.

I get up and we start toward school. Her coat

shrugs up and down with every step. She tries to shove me off the sidewalk with the side of her arm, but I shove back. I shove back all the way.

I can see Goody looking for me from the cafeteria line-up. She's got two orders of fries with gravy on her tray.

I'm nervous about keeping these seats free. I put my coat on one, my knapsack on another and sit down on a third. The hockey guys look at the empty saved chairs but don't say anything. Goody's paying for her food. She looks straight at me and I pat the chair beside me. Serge catches it.

"You two make up?" he asks. If I were less nervous, I'd be loving the scared look on his face.

"Don't worry," I tell him. I stand up and wave for Goody to come. The hockey guys shift in their seats.

I can feel them beginning to hate me. We can't do it without them, though. Being on neutral territory was part of the plan...

There they are. Josie and Tsula walk through the doors. Tsula shifts from one foot to the other. I wave to Goody to come faster. She looks at Josie and rolls her eyes, but she moves in my direction.

"What's going on?" Serge asks.

"You'll see," I say. Josie is laughing. She loves that

I'm making Goody sit with the hockey guys. She loves it because Goody hates it.

"Whatever it is, she's not happy about it," says Serge, watching Goody. Fear shoots off him like practice pucks off the boards.

When Goody reaches the table, I take the knapsack off the seat across from me. She has to get behind Serge's chair to get to the seat and it's too tight a squeeze for her. She looks down at him and glares. The poor guy shrinks his head into his shoulders.

"Goody," I say, reminding her. I watch a chill go up her back. She closes her eyes.

"Excuse me," she says to Serge in her least threatening tone. Serge pulls his chair in and Goody sits down beside him. She pushes up the sleeves of her black sweater and lifts a fry to her mouth, just taking a nibble off the end.

The hockey guys are freaked. It's like Osama bin Laden just sat down to eat with them.

"Gentlemen, please, continue your meals," Goody says and grins at me. I drink in the looks on the hockey guys' faces. I am deeply satisfied. I turn in my chair to look over at Tsula. She's talking to Josie, who looks like she's just been punched in the stomach. I follow Tsula with my eyes as she makes her way to our table. Her lips are pressed together hard. I pull out the chair beside me. Tsula sits and stares down at the table.

"Get another chair. Quick," she says.

Josie is standing in the middle of the cafeteria. She looks lost. Not lost-at-the-airport lost, but lost like lost at sea. Goody pulls a chair from the table behind her and shoves it in beside her. She looks over at Josie and pats it. Josie stares at Tsula, who continues to bore a hole through her lunch tray with her eyes.

Goody raises one eyebrow. I'm beginning to hate her again. Why are we doing this? I forget. I look up to check out Josie, but she's gone. Goody thumbs toward the cafeteria doors. I can see Josie through the glass, making her way down the hall.

"I can't believe you did that," Goody says to Tsula.

"Better be worth it," Tsula tells her.

"Don't worry, pixielocks. I promised Stevie and I keep my promises," Goody says, smirking.

"No," says Tsula. "You don't." The smirk fades off Goody's face and she blushes hot.

Chapter 16

After school, Tsula comes by my locker and tells me that Josie left early.

"I guess she got it," I say. Goody's standing beside me. Tsula looks at her and nods. "She'll come around."

Tsula pushes off without another word. We watch her go down the hall, her books clutched to her chest.

On our way home, I take off toward the park. I'm ready for Goody when she reaches me at the slide platform. She's puffing from trying to catch up. I motion her under the slide to my little fire pit. I reach for my dad's wallet and pull out the swatch. Then I reach under the slide and pull out the other one.

"I didn't know about that one. You little sneak," she says, surprised. Goody's the only one who knows what the swatches mean to me. The last one's in the depression section of the psychology book at school, but I thought I'd keep that one – not for squeaking, but for remembering.

I kneel down in the sand, drop the swatches into the small pit I've dug, get out the matches and light the blue pieces of cloth at the corners. It doesn't take more than a minute for them to burn.

When the swatches are gone, we head out of the park, our feet crunching over the frosty grass. Goody stays quiet. I can feel her brain chewing on what I just did. The smell of the burning cloth still fills my nose. We reach the corner where she turns off and stop.

"You still miss him, don't you?" I nod. "I miss my dad, too. I mean, I have him, and I see him, but I still miss him. I almost wish that I had swatches or something to burn that would make it be like the worst part of missing him was over."

I don't know what to say to that, so I don't say anything. Goody starts down her street, fishing around her gigantic coat pockets for her keys.

When I get home, Mom calls me downstairs. She shows me the black curtain she's hung in front of the darkroom door so that if I want to come in and talk to her while she's working, I can go under the curtain and then through the door. That way no light gets in.

"Help me try it," she says and disappears into the darkroom. I pull the curtain around the door. She's got a piece of cloth up at the top, too, so that no light leaks in there. Once I have the thing pulled around me, I stand in complete darkness, and for a second I feel like I'm invisible. I close my eyes and turn myself around in the small space, then open them.

I don't know where I am.

Mom calls me. I feel around for the doorknob. I open onto a red room. Mom's red teeth are gleaming. She's leaning against a shelf with photography supplies on it. The numbers on the timer float in space just in front of the wall.

I look at my arms. Everything is red.

"It looks like hell," I tell her. Her grin goes wider. "Doesn't it?"

She shows me how she drilled a hole in the wall to put a hose through so that she could have access to water from the laundry room. She's strung wire above Dad's desk so she'll have someplace to hang her photos. She pulls open the filing cabinet and shows me how she's made room for all the pictures she's going to take.

"Now all I need to do is take some shots." She takes me by the hand, opens the door and flips back the curtain. I'm blinded by the sudden light of the basement hallway. I see stars: Sirius, Rigel, Betelgeuse. Mom keeps hold of me up the stairs, sits me down at the kitchen table and gets her camera from the counter.

"Me?" I say as she focuses.

"Of course." My mind flips to the torn photos of Dad that I keep in my wallet. She took those pictures, too. I feel the edge of the wallet – his wallet, my wallet – through my back pocket.

Click. I put my hand in front of my face. Click.

"Wait!" I yell at her. She lowers the camera and looks at me. "Don't you see where I am?" She gets it. She advances the film on the camera.

"Sit up proper and look at me." I take a beat to swallow. Then I sit up proper in my father's chair and let Mom take my picture.

Next day at lunch Goody scoots ahead of me and sits herself down beside Serge who, I swear, looks half happy to see her. I take my seat and watch the door. Josie comes in first. Her eyes dart toward our table and then she makes her way to the cafeteria line-up. Goody's about to go get her fries.

"Wait," I tell her. She sees Josie in the line and stays put. When Tsula comes in, she looks at us and then searches the room for Josie. I point toward the cafeteria line-up. She nods and makes her way over to our table. She takes a seat one away from Goody and doesn't say anything. Josie pays for chips and an apple and stuffs them in her knapsack. Then we all watch her march straight past us and through the cafeteria doors.

Tsula's face falls about a million miles and she makes to go after her. I hold on to her wrist to keep her from leaving, but Goody slaps my hand.

"Let her go," she tells me. Tsula gathers her stuff and runs out the cafeteria doors. Once she's gone, I slap Goody's hand back. She looks down at her hand and then at me. "That was ineffective." I hit it again harder and know as I'm doing it how little it means to her.

"This was my deal, Goody. How come you always have to be the one in charge?" I say to her. She takes in the hockey guys staring at her and bites her lip.

"I wish I knew," she says and digs into her fries.

I stare at her. I don't know why I ever thought I could change anything. Goody's never going to let the plan work. She has to be the one pulling the strings. That's all I am to her – a puppet on a string. Serge and the guys start talking about hockey. I'm too angry to talk to Goody and she knows it and stays quiet. I turn in my seat so my back is facing her and chew my sandwich, wondering if I'll ever get to talk to Tsula again.

"I'm sorry, Stevie," Goody says when the bell rings. I turn around but I still can't look at her. "You finished your whole sandwich," she says. I just nod

and concentrate on scrunching my empty paper bag into a tight ball. "Am I being punished again?"

She stands there waiting for an answer.

"Yes," I say. "Enjoy it." I look up at her and she turns her head away from me. She's not enjoying it. Not one little bit. Good.

Mom's at her photography lesson so I'm alone watching TV when the phone rings a little after seven.

"What did I ever do to you?" Josie's voice cracks at the other end. "I begged her not to do it and she called the cops anyway. And you want me, you all want me to apologize?"

"Would you accept her apology?" I ask. Tsula must have stood up to Josie or she wouldn't be so upset.

"My dad was good. She was jealous of me and him. That's why she did it." I hear her suck in hard.

I walk to the kitchen and turn on the light. The long phone cord trails on the floor beside me.

"I know, Josie. She wants to apologize." I open the fridge and squat in front of it.

"I don't care," she yells.

I find an old cottage cheese container full of meatballs. "I know what Goody's like. She punched me in the stomach," I tell her.

"Why are you her friend then?" she demands. I sit

down in Dad's chair and peel the top off the container. I pick up a meatball, look at it, pop it in my mouth and chew.

"Because she was my friend when I needed one," I say. "I wouldn't have had anyone if it weren't for her." I realize it's true as I'm saying it. "I was pathetic and she put up with that. Man. I think she beat it out of me. You were her best friend once. You know what there is to like about her."

I wait for her to say something or hang up. I can hear her breathing on the other end of the line. I take two meatballs, destroy them and then lick my fingers.

"You don't know what to do, do you?" I say gently.

She hangs up.

I search the cracks in the sidewalk for the right size of stone. I find one and fling it at Goody's window. I look up and wait.

Nothing. I turn into the walkway between the Prynes and their neighbors. I look up at the windows at the side of the house. The lights are off. They go to sleep early. I trip over my foot and stumble into the vinyl siding, making a high-pitched, metal-scraping yeech. I hug the wall and look up at the darkened windows.

Nothing. I go back to looking for stones.

"What do you think you're doing?" It's Goody. She's standing at the gate to her back yard with a blanket wrapped around her and her toque pulled down over her ears. I straighten up and make my way toward her.

"I was looking for stones to throw at your window."

"Aw, Pluto. You're so romantic." She opens the gate and I go through to the picnic table. Sky's clear. I should have figured she'd be out here tonight. I climb up onto the table and sit on the blow-up raft, feel its inflated sides hug up around me. I run my hands along its edges. It's made of swatch material, or something like it. Above me the stars beam down through the branches of the buck-naked trees. Goody once told me that the second dip in Cassiopeia points the way to the Andromeda Galaxy. I look for the smudge and find it.

Goody sits on the bench beside me and winds up her handcrank radio. Through the static I make out the words to "Pinball Wizard." Goody passes me her open bag of Doritos. I shake my head.

"Licorice?" she asks.

"No. That's gone." She uses the radio to pin down the bag of Doritos. When she picks it up the sound comes clearer. "Your mom asleep?" She nods. "It's only 9:30." She shrugs.

"She doesn't want to deal with me, so she goes to bed early."

"My mom's at her photography course. She made a darkroom in Dad's office." I turn my head toward her. She smiles, which is the right thing. She hasn't asked me what I'm doing here. I look back up at the stars. I was going to tell her about Josie calling. I was going to tell her to get her apology ready. "I have one swatch left in the depression book at the library," I tell her and sit up in the raft. "You can have it if you want."

"Why? You going somewhere?" I shake my head and lie back down.

"No, but it feels like I am. How fast is the world turning again?"

"I forget. Fast." I don't believe that she forgets, but I let it slide. "They're going to send me to boarding school, Stevie."

I whip my head sideways. Goody's perfectly calm.

"Don't look like that. I thought this might happen. I told the school counselor that I was having violent fantasies. It wasn't exactly a lie, either. So, of course, they took me to a shrink who suggested family counseling. Like that was going to happen. The next day, Dad sends Mom all these web sites on boarding schools. I'm supposed to go to this one in Peterborough. They take me next week. They couldn't even wait until after Christmas."

Her voice is soft. The song on the radio fades out and I can hear the wind rustling through the plastic of the Dorito package. She wraps the gray blanket more tightly around herself and clears her throat. "My mom says she could use the space to sort some things out. Use the space. Isn't that funny?"

I reach my hand out to her shoulder. She sighs.

"Can't you, like, tell the school counselor on them?" I ask. She shakes her head. "I could get my mom to talk to her about it."

"No. I want to go." She's so calm.

"Why?"

"Because. They want me gone. That money I told you I got? My dad gave me that to go to the movies or the mall on his custody days. He'd pay any amount of money to just get me away. Doesn't matter what I do. They just don't want me around, so that's it. I'm going."

"But you're pugnacious," I say. She laughs.

I lie back and look at the stars. My feet are cold and something's sticking in my back. I dig around back there and pull out binoculars. I put them to my eyes and look up at the Pleiades, a group of sky diamonds that glitter like falling fireworks.

"I don't want you to go," I say, the binoculars still against my eyes.

"That's nice, Stevie. But I think it might be better

for me there. Actually, it's been a good week. It was good you tried to fix things. It doesn't make a difference, though. I'm still going. They told me tonight. I leave this weekend. She's going to miss me. She doesn't think she will, but she's going to."

"Your mom?"

"Yeah. Her, too." I flip on my side and pick up the radio. I crank it up good. It pumps out "Goodbye Yellow Brick Road" by Elton John. It must be an oldies station. Mom has that album. Goody hums along to it a little and I join in near the end. "I'll miss you, Stevie. But you can see how this is kind of like getting to go to another galaxy?"

That's the way it is with Goody. She gets you to go from feeling sorry for her to being jealous of her with a single sentence.

I must have fallen asleep in the blow-up raft, because the next thing I know, Mom's there shaking the car keys over my head. Goody called her.

Chapter 17

Mom can't believe the Prynes are sending Goody to boarding school. It's almost funny how upset she is. She butters her toast so hard the middle comes out. She wanted to call Mrs. Pryne, but I told her what Goody said about how it was kind of like being sent to another galaxy.

"They just don't get her, do they, Stevie?"

I shake my head into my Cheerios and try not to laugh at the way she's holding her toast.

"What's got you so amused? She's your friend." Something in her voice wipes the smile off my face.

I search for my inner black hole but all I can feel is the slosh of milk and Cheerios.

When I get to Skeleton Park, Goody's sitting on the steps to the slide platform. She's got her hair pinned away from her face and that crease in her forehead is all smoothed out. She looks happy.

"Are you all right?" I ask her.

"Yeah, I'm swell. Come on, we've got a lot to do

today." She rumbles down the stairs, hard on her heels.

As we make our way to school, she tells me how she's going to give Josie a letter of apology.

"I was up all night writing it. I want to make a clean break, Stevie, sort everything out before I go. I can't wait to see the look on her face."

"It's a nice letter, right?" I put in. I find myself searching my pockets for pieces of swatch.

"Satisfaction guaranteed." Goody pats my head gently, sending a shiver down my spine.

Something's not right.

"How are you getting to Peterborough?" I ask.

"Dad's driving me."

"What's the school called?"

"Dickinson Academy. It's all girls. It's not really in Peterborough. It's in the country. I bet the place is chock full of cast-offs from dysfunctional families. We'll play dorm games like Who's Got the Most Screws Loose and Pass the Angst."

I relax a bit and we come up with a whole bunch of them: Hide the Gin, How to Hurt Your Sibling So It Doesn't Show, Best Liar Bonanza and, my personal favorite, Say Goodbye to Daddy. That one makes me hysterical. I can't stop picturing Mom tearing up those pictures of Dad. I don't know why it's so funny.

When we get to school, Tsula is standing against the fence.

"Where is that Josie girl?" Goody says. "For two years she's buzzing in my face like a ninety-seven-pound mosquito and now when I want to see her, she's nowhere to be found."

"Can I tell Tsula?" I ask Goody. She nods. "Goody's getting sent to boarding school next week."

Tsula's mouth opens wide enough that I can see her gray gum on her back molars.

"So you see, time is of the essence," says Goody. "When you see Josie, tell her I've got something for her and she can have it right here, at lunch time." Tsula nods and takes off without saying a word.

"She's kind of the opposite of me, isn't she? Is that the attraction, Stevie?"

"I don't know what you're talking about."

I watch Tsula make her way to the front door. She passes Max Revy, who is staring at us from the top of the stairs. I wave to him, and he looks over his shoulder to see who I'm waving at.

I don't see Josie all morning.

When the lunch bell goes, I dash through the hall and out the main doors. Tsula and Josie are standing in the appointed spot. I look around for Goody, but she's nowhere in sight. I don't know what else to do so I go over to them.

"She can forget it," Josie tells me. "I don't want no half-assed apology from her. I'm just here to say good riddance to the fat psycho bitch." I look at Tsula. She looks over my shoulder and juts out her chin.

I take a deep breath and turn my head. Here comes Goody, popsicle cool, envelope in hand. She lumbers up and holds it out to Josie.

Just like that.

"Here," she says, shaking it at her. Josie looks at it skeptically. Her hands are still stuck in the back pockets of her jeans.

"This isn't going to change anything," Josie says.

Tsula takes the envelope from Goody and holds it out to Josie. Goody puts her hands in the pockets of her big-ass coat.

"Open it," Goody says, and her voice is all soft, like I've never heard it.

Josie rips off a corner of the envelope and takes out the piece of paper. She grabs Tsula by the arm and pulls her toward the fence to read it in private.

Josie holds the letter close to her face. I watch her eyes move over the page. Tsula's reading over her shoulder. I turn to look at Goody and she begins to back away.

"Where are you going?" I ask her.

"Home."

"What about school?"

"What are they going to do, suspend me?"

"Don't you want to see what happens?"

"Doesn't matter what she thinks now. I've done all I'm going to do. Anyway, I'll be gone soon."

Goody puts one hand to her forehead and closes her eyes. "I'm bushed, Stevie. I didn't get any sleep last night. Maybe I'll catch you later, okay?" She walks away. A stray bit of her mane hangs loose from her toque and blows behind her.

Josie finishes with the letter and looks over at me. I make my way toward them.

"Where'd she go?" Josie asks.

"Home."

"Really? Couldn't take being nice to me, I guess," Josie says. I don't know what I expected to happen after Goody apologized, but this wasn't it. Josie doesn't seem one bit different.

"There was one part in the letter about you," Tsula tells me. "Show him, Josie."

"Oh, yeah." She digs it out of her pocket and hands it to me. At least she's not treating me like I'm the enemy anymore. They both look over my shoulder as Tsula points out the spot. *Please treat Stevie nice after I'm gone. He's good.*

"She's so weird," I say. Josie slaps my arm with the back of her hand.

"She's a freak, little man. You ought to know that by now. Don't worry, though. I'll be nice. Right, Tsula? At least, I'll be as nice to you as Goody was." She slaps me again.

Tsula smiles at me with her gold eyes, and it's like they're throwing off heat, because I'm getting all warm.

The fluorescent lights of the library hum over me as I go through the turnstile. I go to the shelf and look for my psychology book. I flip through the depression section until I find my last swatch. I pull out my wallet and put it in.

I'll give it to Goody tonight. I can just see her framing it for her desk at boarding school.

Just as I'm about to leave, something catches my eye. I turn and look at Goody's usual spot. Her astronomy book is there. I pick it up and run my fingers over the author's name at the bottom of the cover.

Terence Dickinson.

I'm still holding the book when the bell rings.

I float through my afternoon classes daydreaming about how my life is going to change. I'll sit with the hockey guys at lunch. I'll write to Goody at boarding school and tell her all about how Serge chews with his mouth open. Maybe Tsula will sit beside me, like Bea sits beside Kent. Maybe I'll take her down to Mom's darkroom and…develop things.

All the way home, I'm thinking about developing things with Tsula, so I'm on automatic when I reach into our mailbox and pull out the parcel. I walk into the front hall and tear the brown paper off it.

It's Goody's log book.

I open it. On the inside of the front cover is a note to me.

Stevie: Something to remember me by. Love, Goody.

My inner black hole springs open and gasps for air. I march to the phone, dial Goody's number and pace the kitchen as it rings six times. No answer. No machine. I let it ring three more times before I give up. I ransack the living room in search of the phone book. It's crammed behind the cushion on the recliner. I take it to the kitchen table and look up the number for the Queen's University registrar's office. I get the number wrong the first time and have to dial again. Slowly. Carefully.

I don't know what I'm going to say.

One ring. A lady answers and I ask for Mrs. Pryne. She tells me to wait a minute.

"Can I help you?"

It's her. I have to say something.

"Hi, Mrs. Pryne. It's Stevie Walters."

"Hello, Steven. You've called my office."

Think.

"I know. I...I was thinking of doing a surprise for Goody, but I need the address of that place." Keep cool. Just need to know.

"What place is that?" she asks blankly. I can hear her still working her keyboard.

My heart begins to bang against the back of my throat. I pick up the log book and strum through the star-dotted pages, panicking.

"In Peterborough? That school." I hear noises in the background, the keyboard and shuffling papers.

"What school?" Her voice is louder in the receiver now.

"Where she's going." I swallow hard. "Dickinson Academy?" The background noises stop. "I'm sorry, Mrs. Pryne. I think I made a mistake."

"She told you she was changing schools?"

"No. No. I must have heard her wrong. It's all right. Never mind." I put my hand over the receiver and curse.

"Steven, are you there? What did my daughter tell you?" her voice pleads as I hang up.

I shove the log book in my pocket as I head out the door.

All the way to Goody's house I'm putting pieces together.

I'm making my way up the front steps when Mrs. Pryne pulls in the driveway. I pound on the front door. Mrs. Pryne gets out of the car and fumbles through her keys.

"Here," she says, squeezing past me. I hold open the screen door for her as she trembles the key into the lock.

"Goody?" she calls when she gets it open.

"I phoned but there was no answer," I say. Mrs. Pryne gets this horrible look on her face. She races upstairs and I stumble up after her. She's knocking on Goody's closed door as I get to the top.

"I'll do it," I tell her and make to move past her.

Goody opens the door. Her mother leans against the wall, half laughing, half crying.

"What?" Goody asks me. Her eyes are all puffy. "I was asleep."

Three minutes later we're sitting around Goody's kitchen table drinking water out of tall clear glasses full of ice.

"I swear, I was just tired, Mom. I turned the phone down. I didn't think anyone would call. You didn't have to rush home." Mrs. Pryne seems about ready to accept this, so I push the log book onto the kitchen table. Goody gives me a warning look, but I plunge on.

"She gave this to me," I tell her mother. "She said you and Mr. Pryne were sending her to boarding school."

"He's lying – " Goody tries to talk over me, but I have Mrs. Pryne's full attention.

"This weekend is when she said she was going. She said Mr. Pryne was driving her. Why would I lie?" Mrs. Pryne and Goody stare at each other.

"She said the boarding school was called Dickinson Academy. That's how I thought it might be fake. Dickinson's the last name of the guy who wrote her favorite astronomy book. Look at this." I open the front cover of the log book and push it across the table.

Mrs. Pryne reads the note Goody wrote to me and bites her lip, just like Goody does. Goody's head hangs forward so I can't see her face through all the hair in front of it.

"Where were you going to go, Goody?" her mother asks. The kitchen light is off. Afternoon shadows cut shapes into the kitchen counter. Mrs. Pryne scrapes her chair sideways, closer to Goody. She sits there for a minute, waiting. Then she lifts her hand and brushes Goody's cheek with it.

Goody looks sideways at me through wet eyes, then turns into her mother and bursts.

"Away," she says. "Way, way away."

When I get home, the picture Mom took of me in the kitchen the other day is sitting in the middle of the table.

"Where've you been? I've got supper waiting on you."

"Out," I say. I'll tell her later. I sit down and peel my sweater off onto the back of the chair and pull the picture toward me. In it, I'm wearing my new clothes, in Dad's seat. Bright sunlight crosses one side of my face and my straight mouth.

I look older than I thought. Taller.

"What do you think?" she says, moving from the stove to bend over me. "Do you think it needs more contrast?" She picks it up and takes a closer look.

"It's good, Mom."

"You look like him, you know."

"Do I?" She puts the picture back down on the table.

"Yup." She pushes off my shoulder and goes back to the stove. The room's full of stew smell. When it hits the bowl, I pull it closer and let the steam of it heat my face.

Dumplings.

Chapter 18

Goody's mom pulled her out of school for a while. I'm picking up her homework for her, probably until the new year. Everyone at school's been told she's got mononucleosis.

Mrs. Pryne gave me a key so I let myself in. Goody's lying on the couch staring out the window.

"Squeak," she says as I walk in.

"How'd it go today?" I ask.

"The shrink doesn't tell me how it's going. But he said I could opt out of exams this term. If anyone asks, tell them that's how I planned it. I went crazy to get out of exams. They'll buy that."

"No problem," I say. "But you aren't really crazy." I put the books down on the coffee table and sit cross-legged on the floor. I notice the white rug hasn't been vacuumed in a while.

"I don't know, Stevie. I was on my way to another galaxy. Dad was here this weekend. You want to know what he said?" I shake my head. "He said, 'There goes Christmas,' like I'd killed Santa Claus."

"What's Christmas got to do with it?"

"Nothing. Christmas has nothing to do with it. Maybe he had plans with his girlfriend. I don't know. That's the other thing he told me. They're getting married. She's going to be my stepmother. I wonder if he'll still give me money to stay away after they're married?"

Goody bites her big lip. The side of her neck is covered in shadow. A good contrast shot, Mom would say.

"I can take it, though. I'm pugnacious, right? Actually, it's more like I'm seven pugnacious people and we're all packed in here – " Goody knocks her forehead. She props herself up on one elbow and smooths the afghan on top of her. "Where do other people keep themselves, Stevie? Why aren't they as big as me?"

I shake my head and look out the window. The snow makes eddies in the air above the street.

"I wish I were as big as you, Goody. On the inside, I mean." She sighs and kicks me in the shoulder with her foot. She's smiling.

"You make the absolute worst wishes."

Before I leave, I go up to the bathroom. I go to

Goody's room and take out my wallet. I pull out my swatch and rub it against my cheek one last time. I lift Goody's mattress and stick the swatch under it. Then I smooth out her comforter, go to the bathroom and flush the toilet.

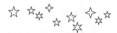

Two weeks later. It's almost December. I'm raking leaves into piles and Tsula's stuffing the piles into plastic bags. The lady customer is watching us from her kitchen window.

"She's afraid we might steal a couple of leaves," says Tsula.

I laugh. The leaves are edged with frost. I've got the arms of my sweater pulled over my hands to keep them warm, and I've got blisters on my thumbs from all the raking we've been doing.

It's not so bad. Tsula, Josie and I started coming to this fancy neighborhood because the yards are bigger and we can charge more. The people here tip, too. We've only been doing this six days and I'm already up to $96. It's too bad we started so late. There's hardly any leaves left.

It was weird raking with Josie at first. She's very polite to me now, and even jokes around sometimes. She even asks me about Goody and how she's doing. She and Tsula are the only ones who know what really happened with her. I had to tell them everything because Josie went over to Goody's to work things out with her and found the house empty. I figured if Josie was ready to work things out, then she deserved to know the truth.

Last Wednesday, when Tsula was carrying bags of leaves to the front of a house, Josie told me that she could see why Goody chose me as a friend.

"You, too," I said, and we both went back to raking.

Josie's visiting her dad today so it's just me and Tsula. It was Josie's idea we should rake leaves for money. She came up with the idea when we were talking about Goody's Arizona fund. Josie wants to buy her dad this fancy wooden photo box for Christmas. Tsula's going to save up to buy her own laptop. I think I might use my money to get my own camera. Mom's showing me how to develop black-and-white film.

The other good thing about raking leaves is that it's building up my muscles. Oh, sure, they're just little leaf muscles now, but you can see them moving in there. I like being outside where I can see far away. I like the smell of the leaves and the sound of the rake. I like hanging out with Tsula and Josie.

I got a postcard from Goody yesterday. It had a picture of a cactus on the front, but the back was all about the stars. She and her mom are renting a cabin near the Grand Canyon. It's not tourist season, so they have the place pretty much to themselves. Goody wrote that they're both getting pains in the neck from looking at the sky. She's teaching her mom all about the constellations.

"These leaves are cold and crusty," I tell Tsula.

"They're poking holes in the garbage bags. Won't be long before they're all gone. At least then we won't have to do this anymore," she says.

I look at my hands and squeak them together.

"You don't like this? I don't mind. I wish it were last week so we could still do this for a couple of more weeks."

"You are so strange," says Tsula, packing the leaves down with her knee.

I take a deep breath and hold it, watching the way the light hits the yard's long wooden fence. I take a picture of it with my brain, knowing it will leak out of my memory five minutes from now.

"Yeah, that was a stupid wish," I say, and I can hear Goody's voice in my head.

I wish I had a picture of me and Goody. That's something I want frozen and safe and with me forever. A little piece of before, so I can remember these past two years – when I was sad and Goody Pryne was my best friend.